# TURMOIL ON THE THAMES

# Also by Marissa Doyle

## The Ladies of Almack's series

*The Forgery Furore*
*The Vanishing Volume*
*Lyrics and Larceny*
*The Cursed Canvases*
*Turmoil on the Thames*
*An Event at Epsom (August 2022)*
*The Missing Missives (September 2022)*

*Skin Deep*
*By Jove*

## The Leland Sisters series

*Bewitching Season*
*Betraying Season*
*Courtship and Curses*
*Charles Bewitched*

*Between Silk and Sand*
*Evergreen*
*What Lies Beneath*

# TURMOIL ON THE THAMES

## THE LADIES OF ALMACK'S
## BOOK 5

# Marissa Doyle

In association with
Book View Cafe

TURMOIL ON THE THAMES: A LIGHT-HEARTED REGENCY FANTASY (THE LADIES OF ALMACK'S BOOK 5)
Copyright © 2022 Marissa Doyle

All rights reserved. No part or the whole of this book may be reproduced, distributed, transmitted, or utilized (other than for reading by the intended reader) in any form without the prior written permissions of the author, except in the case of brief quotations embodied in critical reviews and certain other non-commercial uses permitted by copyright law. The unauthorized reproduction of this copyrighted work is illegal, and punishable by law.

Published by Book View Café LLC
304 S. Jones Blvd., Suite #2906
Las Vegas, NV 89107

ISBN: 978-1-63632-049-6

This is a work of fiction. Names, characters, places, and events are fictitious and/or are used fictitiously and are solely the product of the author's imagination. Any similarity to real persons, living or dead, places, businesses, companies, institutions, events, or locales is completely coincidental.

https://www.bookviewcafe.com

https://www.marissadoyle.com

For Scott,
who kept asking for what happened next

# Chapter One

*Chesterfield Street, London
Early June 1810*

Annabel knew she was being shameless. Indeed, she was quite certain her behavior verged on decadence. And she was enjoying every minute of it.

She lifted the spoonful of sliced strawberries dripping with sugared cream to her lips. Ah, heaven. Now a sip of chocolate, accompanied by a blissful wriggling of her toes under the counterpane. Lying abed till half-past ten whilst drinking chocolate and eating strawberries and cream was abandoned behavior indeed for a Shellingham. Thank goodness the portrait hanging over the chimneypiece of Grandmama—given last year as a special mark of her approval of Annabel's continued chaste widowhood—was just canvas and paint. Poor Grandmama would be scandalized if she truly were present.

But really, didn't she deserve a half-hour or so of regret-free dissipation? Last week's investigation of the mysterious alterations to the pictures at the

Royal Academy's Summer Exhibition had been especially tiring, both physically and emotionally. She'd *earned* a little relaxation this morning. And this afternoon—she smiled in anticipation.

Today was the Fourth of June and the birthday of the dear old king. While few people outside court circles would pay much attention to the date, in one place it would be celebrated as a high holiday.

Because of its proximity to Windsor Castle, the king's favorite residence, Eton College and its students had always enjoyed a firm friendship with his majesty. The king took a deep personal interest in the school and was a frequent visitor, and Eton's boys responded by turning his birthday into an unofficially official day of celebration. The "unofficially" part was because the headmaster and staff of Eton did not sanction or participate (at least openly) in the day's events, turning an indulgently blind eye to the annual boat race—ahem, procession—upon the Thames, followed by a picnic and evening fireworks.

Their presence wasn't missed. The event had become part of the social season, and the *ton* turned out in force for it even if Eton's masters didn't. Dukes and earls and even the king's own sons came to be taken as guests on the boys' boats and to drink champagne in the field across from Surly Hall, a well-known riverside pub, where the race ended.

Today Annabel would be among their number, for Will and Martin had demanded that she come—bringing a suitably magnificent picnic, of course—to join them for their first Fourth of June.

Annabel had agreed at once; in another year or two her presence might not be so welcome. She and her cook had conferred over the contents of the picnic box last week after Martin sent another note entreating her to bring *lots* of sandwiches and cakes—especially his favorite iced cakes that only Mrs. Dailey could bake.

Annabel smiled at the memory of her son's earnest note. In a little while she would rise and dress and pay a visit to the kitchen to see how Mrs. Dailey was getting on. Or. . . or perhaps she'd just pour herself another cup of chocolate and—

An urgent scratch at her dressing room door made her sit up. Before she could respond, her maid Winters had thrown open the door, her pale face even paler than usual. "Madam!" she gasped. "Lord and Lady Shellingham are here!"

"What?" Annabel stared at her. Mama and Papa here in London, at this time of year? "Right now? Where are they?"

"Hanscomb put them in the salon and is bringing them coffee." Winters hurried to remove the tray from Annabel's lap. "Lady Shellingham says she will come up to see you in a few minutes. I have your water for washing."

"Oh, heavens!" Annabel jumped out of bed. So much for her peaceful morning in bed! What could have brought her parents to London? Papa hated being away from Belsever Magna in spring and only came to town when there was a question being discussed in Parliament that he cared about. Perhaps that was it—but why hadn't they told her they were coming?

With Winters' help she was washed and hastily arrayed in a dressing gown when a firm knock sounded on her door and Mama's voice called, "Annabel?"

"Mama!" Annabel rose from her dressing table as Winters opened the door. "What a lovely surprise!"

Sarah, Lady Shellingham was a small, plump woman with dreamy blue eyes whose vague manner was completely spurious—except when it wasn't. "Is it?" she said. "Didn't the boys tell you we'd be coming with you to Eton today? We got the sweetest letter from Will begging us to come."

"No, they didn't—not that I'm not delighted to see you." Annabel bent to kiss her mother's soft cheek.

"Well, since the new barouche he ordered was ready and his roses were still a week from their full display, your father thought we could manage a few days in London. We came down Friday. We're staying at Grillon's—it didn't make sense to open the house just for a few days—"

"You could have stayed with me," Annabel interrupted reproachfully.

"No, we couldn't. Papa was afraid you'd try to make him go to Almack's."

"But Almack's is only on Wednesdays."

"I know, dear, but he doesn't always listen. I don't know what we'll do next year when little Sarah is ready to make her curtsey to the queen. Your sister will want us here in town, of course, but tearing Papa from his roses will be next to impossible." Mama sighed and took off her hat, then seated herself at Annabel's dressing table to pat her hair smooth. "You aren't still wearing that disgraceful thing, are you?" she added, glancing at Annabel through the mirror.

Annabel flushed. Her dressing gown was old—and looked it. "It's not as if anyone ever sees me in it but Winters."

"*I'm* seeing it, right now. . . and you never know who else might at some point."

"Mama!" Annabel could not decide whether to be scandalized or amused.

Mama turned away from the mirror and peered more closely at her. "You do look tired, darling. Perhaps you need to cut down on your social commitments? I shall have a word with Sally Jersey before we go home. If Almack's is wearing you down this much—"

"Mama, I'm not twelve! And anyway, it's not that—" Annabel began, then stopped. Mama of course had no idea about her extra duties with the Lady Patronesses. "This was just a—an especially busy week."

"Hmm." Mama turned back to the mirror, this time carefully *not* looking at her. "Are there, ah, any specific persons keeping you busy of late?"

Annabel restrained a sigh. For the last year and a half Mama had been dropping both delicate and not-so-delicate hints about her marital status, or lack thereof. Unlike Grandmama Shellingham, she thought it long past time for Annabel to remarry.

She opened her mouth to reply in the negative to Mama's question, then stopped. Someone *had* been occupying a great deal of her attention—two someones, in fact. But she winced at the idea of telling her mother about Lord Glenrick's kissing her. And Lord Quinceton of course did not even belong in this conversation, no matter how much time she had recently spent in his company. "If anyone begins to keep me busy in that fashion, Mama, you shall know at once," she said with a bright smile.

"Oh, darling." Mama shook her head. "You are still the worst liar in all England, aren't you? Who is he?"

How did Mama always know? She hesitated, then said, "Um—Lord Glenrick. He's been, ah, most attentive."

Mama gave up any pretense of primping at the mirror and turned in her seat to face her. "Glenrick? Good heavens!"

Annabel looked away. "He seems to think me attractive."

Mama waved her hand. "Of course he does. You're a very attractive girl. But haven't you paid any attention—no, I don't suppose you have over the last few years. Everyone knows that the Carricks are practically at a standstill and that Glenrick would be a fool if he married anyone but an heiress to shore up the family fortunes. Regrettably, you are *not* an heiress. So why is he dangling after you, unless—" She frowned. "Has he tried to kiss you?"

"Er, yes."

Mama's frown deepened. "In that case, I expect he wants to make you his mistress. There's nothing wrong with that if it is agreeable to you, so long as you're discreet about it. However, considering how quickly you were breeding after you married Freddy, I would worry about unintended consequences—"

"Goodness, Mama!" Being a Shellingham for forty years had not repressed her mother's straightforwardness.

"—still, I could wish better for you." She sighed. "Papa and I *would* be pleased to see you married again." She rose and wandered over to the window. "I had hoped Freddy was going to be a better husband than he turned out to be. He seemed to quite dote upon you when he asked us for your hand, which was why Papa agreed to overlook the fact that his finances weren't as solid as we would have preferred."

Annabel looked sadly at her back. "It—it all turned out well enough, Mama. I have Will and Martin, after all."

"True." Mama's shoulders relaxed—but not entirely. "Speaking of whom, isn't it time you were dressed? We have an enormous picnic waiting in the carriage for two hungry little boys."

Annabel paused on her way to ring for Winters. "What? Did they ask you for food as well?"

Mama laughed and turned from the window. "The way Will phrased it, they're positively wasting away. I expect they'll grow six inches over the summer. Your brothers were the same way—two months of insatiable appetite, and then I had to order all new clothes for them because they'd outgrown everything in their wardrobes."

"I hope they're getting enough to eat,"

Annabel said. Was Mrs. Poltrey, who ran their lodging, feeding them properly? They had looked well enough when they were home at Easter, but perhaps this was a more recent problem. She would have to question them this afternoon. She went to the bell and rang for Winters.

"Annabel." Mama had followed her; now she touched her arm. "About Glenrick. Do you return his regard?"

Annabel paused, still holding the bell pull. Did she? She had been so wrapped up in being flattered by his obvious preference and by Frances's marital hints that she hadn't truly considered that question. She thought of his kiss on that quiet wooded path at Hampton Court and what she'd felt—or not felt.

"I don't know," she said, looking down at the toes of her slippers. "I can't help feeling a little—well, he's the next Duke of Carrick, after all. And I've never felt *desired* before. I hadn't realized what a heady sensation that could be. But now, thinking about it without him before me—I don't know."

"Oh, my poor dear." Mama folded her in an embrace. "I could just *smite* your lout of a husband."

Annabel had been inclined to teariness, but Mama's indignation made her laugh instead. "That's already happened if you recall—the poor old dear. And I'm quite well. Just. . . confused."

"Men. The world would be a much simpler place without them, wouldn't it, Winters?" Annabel's maid had appeared, bearing a bronze muslin walking dress trimmed with bands of brown silk.

"That it would, your ladyship." Winters had

been a maid at Belsever Magna before becoming Annabel's maid. "Perhaps not as amusing, however."

"I'll take simple over amusing any day," Mama said firmly. "Is that a new dress?"

"No, an old one we remade. Don't you care for it? I think it's one of Winters' best efforts." Annabel smiled at her maid. "One does not dress up too much for this event, so I understand."

"Hmm." Mama eyed the dress as Winters laced Annabel's stays and helped her on with a petticoat. "Very pretty, but—" She pressed her lips together and said, more firmly, "Very pretty."

Mama herself was, as always, beautifully turned out, today in cream-colored muslin with a high-necked lilac sarsenet mantle. Annabel knew that her straitened circumstances and limited dress allowance troubled her fashionable parent, but Mama had sufficient delicacy to not make too great a fuss about it.

While Winters dressed her hair in a simple style, Mama wandered around the room, examining her treasures: miniatures of the boys when they were three by Richard Cosway, a pair of Limoges vases Freddy had given her when the boys were born, the small but exquisite watercolor of an orchid that the boys' friend Augustus Blackburn—Gus—had painted for her.

"That's a pretty thing," Mama commented, peering at it closely.

"Isn't it? You'll probably have the opportunity to meet the artist later today." Gus would almost certainly be there with the boys this afternoon—or at least with Martin, while Will rowed.

"I'll look forward to it—good heavens, darling!" Mama said, pausing before the portrait of Grandmother Shellingham. "Do you really want a picture of Grandmama in your *bedchamber*?"

"Why? What's wrong with it?"

"It's so—unconducive!"

Winters gave a strangled sort of cough but heroically maintained her countenance; upper servants never betrayed that they'd heard a word uttered by their superiors unless directly addressed. Annabel, however, had no such constraints. "Mama!"

Mama shrugged. "All I can say, dear, is that if I'd allowed your grandmother's portrait in *my* bedchamber, you and your brothers and sister might not be here today. Poor Papa!" She surveyed it a moment longer, then shook her head.

"How is Grandmama, anyway?"

"Oh, very well. There are still fifteen chairs in the dining room that need new covers. I think she's signed a pact with the devil to stay alive until she's done embroidering them."

Annabel grinned. Why didn't that surprise her? Grandmama sometimes seemed to forget that her eldest son was himself a grandfather now.

"You're ready, milady," Winters said, setting down her comb and handing Annabel her earrings.

"Thank you, Winters." Annabel slipped them on. "Speaking of Papa, shall we go down and join him for coffee before he thinks we've forgotten him?" She stood up, took Mama's arm, and led her from the room. As the door closed behind her, she heard poor Winters giving way to her pent-up mirth and smiled in sympathy.

Two hours later, after not only coffee but a hastily-improvised nuncheon Annabel called for after Papa's pointed complaints about the inadequacy of breakfast at their hotel, they were off to Eton in Annabel's landau.

That had taken some negotiating. Just the day before, Papa had taken delivery of a new barouche of which he was very proud, lacquered in the Shellingham maroon and gray and with new matching liveries for his coachman and groom that he had designed himself. But Mama had put her dainty lilac kid half-boot down and declared that they would drive with Annabel. "I have not seen my daughter in months," she said firmly, "and I intend to drive with her. You may take the new barouche, but you will look very silly being driven to Eton all alone, no matter how much you want to show it off."

Papa glowered. "I don't want to show it off. I want to ascertain that all is as it should be before we drive it home. *A stitch in time saves nine.*"

"Nonsense. You and Ambrose drove it around London for an hour and a half yesterday. If there were something wrong with it that required the carriage-maker's attention, you would have found it then." She fixed him with a stern look. "*Pride goeth before a fall.*"

He sighed. "Your point, Sarah."

Annabel tried not to smile. Mama lately had taken to countering Papa's beloved maxims with her own, often more aptly chosen. She twined her arm in his as Mama rang for Hanscomb to have the carriage brought around. "I'm glad we're going all together, Papa," she said, and kissed his cheek.

He continued to glower despite the corners of his mouth having turned up. "Trying to turn me up sweet, are you, you artful puss? Well, I won't have it." But he squeezed her arm and sent the new barouche back to the hotel's stables and climbed into the landau without demur when Thomas drove it up. "Do we have quite enough food, d'ye think?" he commented, eyeing the large wicker hamper in the seat next to him. A similar hamper had been stowed in the boot, along with a folding table and campaign stools to sit on.

"I hope so." Annabel adjusted her sunshade; the early afternoon sun was bright. "The boys were emphatic about it."

He folded his hands on the expanse of waistcoat covering his comfortable belly. "*Man cannot live by bread alone*."

Mama snorted. "*Boys will be boys*."

Papa tried to frown but failed. "They will, won't they? Your point, my dear."

"Yes, I know. Now, Annabel, perhaps you know—what is this dreadful story we've heard about the Duke of Cumberland? Did his valet really try to murder him?"

"That's what they're saying. I haven't heard much else," Annabel said. The gossip had begun circulating on Thursday that the king's fifth son, the

Duke of Cumberland, had been attacked and nearly killed by one of his valets, a Sardinian named Joseph Sellis, that previous night. But she had been in the thick of the Summer Exhibition investigation and had not paid much attention to the whole sordid matter.

"Doesn't surprise me in the least. Cumberland's a bad 'un," Papa said. "Always has been. Of course, that's not to say he deserved to be attacked in his bed in the middle of the night. And the valet slit his own throat, it seems. They say Cumberland had been far too friendly with the man's wife. Or with Sellis himself. Place looked as if a pig had been slaughtered in it, evidently."

"Really, George, must we?" Mama wrinkled her nose. "I wondered what had you as thick as thieves with our waiter at breakfast. You were gossiping."

"I was gathering information," Papa said loftily. "Men don't gossip."

Mama snorted. *"Heed not what a man says, but what he does."*

"How are your roses faring, Papa? Did they survive the winter unscathed?" Annabel asked before he had finished sputtering. Talking about his roses was guaranteed to divert Papa from just about anything.

It worked. Papa happily spent the next hour discussing each of his bushes in detail, including the number of buds set in some cases. Annabel privately resolved to have the boys invite Gus to Belsever Magna during one of their summer holiday visits to paint a few of his favorites.

As they approached the village of Eton, the roads grew crowded. Papa sighed as he waved to the sixth carriageful of his acquaintances, and Annabel knew he was regretting not having taken his new barouche. She saw many acquaintances of her own and was pleasantly surprised when a carriage containing Maria Sefton, Lord Sefton, and a pair of gentlemen pulled alongside them.

"Annabel!" Maria exclaimed. "I'd wondered if you would be here to visit the boys." She smiled and nodded at Mama. "Lady Shellingham, it's a pleasure to see you."

"Yes—Will is rowing." Annabel couldn't keep a note of pride out of her voice.

"Oh, that's splendid. I'm glad to see one of us here," she added in a slightly lower voice. "There's something I might need your help with—"

"Hoy, Shellingham! Where's this new barouche I've heard about?" Lord Sefton boomed, drowning out his wife's words.

Papa smiled through gritted teeth. "I'd be happy to take you around Hyde Park in it tomorrow, sir."

"That's done it," Mama murmured to Annabel. "We'll be in London till your father's done showing off his barouche to all and sundry."

"Ha! I should enjoy that, sir! Drive on!" Lord Sefton called to his coachman.

"I'll find you after the procession!" Maria called as their coach drew ahead.

"I shall look for you," Annabel replied, but they had already passed. What might Maria need her help with? It must be special Lady Patroness business, or she wouldn't have been so circumspect. Heavens, was there a new investigation looming already?

In another half hour they'd finally reached the Brocas, a large, south-facing meadow directly on the Thames with a lovely view of the towers of Windsor Castle to the southeast. Thomas left them off near the road to make their way toward the river where the race would be starting. The field looked so cheerful, its green breadth milling with excited boys (some on horseback) and strolling sightseers, that Annabel regretted that they could not picnic right here on the sunny grass. But any such thoughts were banished by the sight of the Honourable Martin Chalfont running toward them at full tilt, his beaver hat in hand.

"You're here!" he shouted and flung himself at her. Before she could begin to give him the briefest of hugs, he'd already caromed off her like an errant billiard ball to give his grandparents a similar greeting. "Did you bring a *huge* picnic?" he demanded.

"Yes, two of them, you jackanapes!" Annabel answered. "Why didn't you say you'd written to your grandparents as well?"

He looked at her as if he doubted her intellectual capacity. "Because I wanted them to come and bring a picnic too. Twice as much. I *can* do maths, you know."

"Isn't Mrs. Poltrey giving you enough to eat?" Annabel examined his figure anxiously. He didn't look particularly thinner—

"Oh, yes, she feeds us good and proper. We

just wanted a bang-up feast today." He grinned up at her angelically.

A faint warning bell sounded in Annabel's mind. She knew that grin. . .and from experience, distrusted it.

"Where is your brother, Martin?" Mama asked before she could question him further.

"Oh, down by the boats. Gus is somewhere too. You'll see 'em at Surly's after the race. Give me a minute to gather everything, and we can get going. Where are your carriages?"

"What 'everything' requires gathering?" Annabel asked.

His smile remained, but his gaze slithered away from hers. "Just a few things we wanted to bring along."

Annabel looked past her offspring and saw a quintet of boys who bore a strong resemblance to pack donkeys, loaded with what appeared to be several planks, four sawhorses, and a bundle of tall naphtha torches. "What do you need those—"

"Can I go with *you*, Grandpapa?" Martin interrupted, inserting just the right note of hero worship in his voice.

Predictably, Papa melted. "I should say you can—except I doubt there'll be room enough in your mother's carriage what with the extra picnic hamper—"

"You came together?" For the first time, Martin's smile faltered. "But how am I supposed to get our stuff there?"

"Martin, what is all this for?" Annabel asked in a firm voice.

"Just for—for a thing we're doing tonight. It's—it's in honor of the king's birthday," he added, with the air of a relieved magician who finds he has not flubbed his trick after all. "I didn't know you'd be coming in just one carriage, though. You should have said so!"

Papa examined Martin's retinue with a practiced eye. "You might fit all that in your mother's carriage if none of us had come," he said. "No notion how you'll get it there, my boy."

"But I have to!" Martin's face crumpled, and he seemed alarmingly close to tears.

"It is very simple," a familiar voice said from behind Annabel. "Lord and Lady Shellingham will drive in my curricle with my groom, and Fellbridge and I shall walk to Surly's. The river path is only a couple of miles. That will leave the landau to Master Chalfont and his, er, accoutrements."

## Chapter Two

Of course. She should have *known* he would turn up here today. "This is an unexpected, er, pleasure, sir," Annabel said as she turned to face the speaker.

Lord Quinceton swept off his hat. She just caught the mischievous gleam in his eyes before he made her a low bow. "A pleasure indeed. But I don't see why it should be so unexpected, as I happen to be an Old Boy myself." He bowed again to Mama. "Your servant, Lady Shellingham. Sir," he added, nodding to Papa.

"How d'ye do, Quinceton," Papa greeted him affably. Of course Papa was acquainted with him from the House of Lords.

Martin fixed Lord Quinceton with a suspicious stare. "Who're you?"

"I don't presume to call myself a friend of your mother's, Master Chalfont, but perhaps I can lay claim to being her devoted acquaintance," he replied. "I am Quinceton."

Annabel snorted. "You, sir, presume precisely as much as you want, when you want."

"I beg you not to speak so, madam! You'll give your family a bad impression of me." He shook his head in mock distress.

"No worse than the one you're giving yourself. You're being quite ridiculous, you know." And so was she. No, the day was *not* suddenly brighter and more exciting just because he had arrived. Not in the least.

"My apologies." He inclined his head. "I've told you before, you do bring out the worst in me."

"Only because you permit it!"

"But the temptation, Fellbridge! The temptation!" Did he have to smile at her in that fashion, so that the corners of her own mouth could only turn up in response?

Martin was not satisfied. "Why'd you call my mother Fellbridge? That's my brother's name."

"It is indeed—or it will be when he's old enough to do it honor," Lord Quinceton said, now all seriousness. "In the meanwhile, your mother is performing that task heroically."

"Hmm," Mama said to no one in particular.

Papa appeared much impressed by this statement. "By God, she is, isn't she? Since Freddy was fool enough to cock up his toes as he did, he should be deucedly grateful to have married someone who was able to pick up the pieces he left behind. Thank you for the offer of your curricle, Quinceton, but I believe I fancy a walk as well. What do you think, my dear?"

Martin's face uncrumpled. "Then *I* can drive the carriage there?"

"No, you may not, young man. Thomas will drive you," Annabel said firmly. She turned to Mama. "Unless you would care to go with him?"

"No, I shall walk as well," she said. "It *is* a lovely day, and if I grow tired, your father will carry me."

"What?" Papa's eyes widened.

Mama smiled at him sweetly and took his arm. "Come along, dear. We'll see you all soon!" She propelled him gently toward the river.

"Fellbridge?" Lord Quinceton murmured. That mischievous twinkle was back.

Too late she realized that she'd fallen in with his plan without even having considered otherwise. "Oh, very well," she said, perhaps not as graciously as she ought. The man was possibly even better than her mother at arranging situations to his liking. "I must tell Thomas that he should drive Martin and his friends. Would Gus care to go with you?" she asked her son.

Martin shot one more suspicious look at Lord Quinceton, then shook his head vigorously. "No, he can't. No room," he added, at her surprised look. "Come on, men!" He began to march toward the road, leading his crew of boys in the manner of a nabob with his retinue of native bearers.

Once the doubting Thomas had been assured that yes, she really did want him to drive Martin and his baggage to the field opposite Surly Hall and that she herself truly did want to walk there, Annabel took Lord Quinceton's proffered arm and allowed him to lead her toward the river to see the boats. The sun sparkled on the water, but a soft breeze kept its warmth from becoming oppressive. "I will admit that it is a perfect day for a walk," she said as they strolled down the field.

"That is what I appreciate about you, Fellbridge—one thing among others, I should say. You're always gracious in defeat."

"I was not aware there had been a contest."

"Perhaps not a contest, but I concede that I did rather take over your plans for the day. Well, your son and I. However, everyone seems content with the results. At least I hope they are." He glanced at her sideways.

"Surely the fact that *you* are is enough?"

Instead of laughing and agreeing, which was what she expected him to do, he shook his head. "No, not at all. Do you take me for such a selfish fellow?"

"I take you for one determined to get what he wants."

"Fair enough. At least you are forewarned."

Annabel felt herself color and was grateful for the concealing brim of her hat. "Why didn't you say you were coming today when I mentioned I would be here?" she asked, to change the subject.

"Does it perturb you that I did come?"

"Are you waiting for me to say, 'Fie, Lord Quinceton, indeed I am delighted to see you here!'"

He grinned. "It would be gratifying if you would. I didn't say I would be here because I was not yet certain that I would be. I did not know whether you were coming with Glenrick and couldn't think of a delicate way to ask. It is not much of a pleasure to see you in his company."

He was determined to make her blush today, wasn't he? "Confessing yourself at a loss? I *am* astonished, sir!"

"You're supposed to be. It's all part of my fiendishly devious plan to keep you off balance."

She looked up at him, truly astonished this time. "Why do you want to do that?"

He smiled. "I am somewhat surprised my lord Glenrick did not undertake to accompany you today," was all he said.

Ah. So he was in one of *those* moods. She would endeavor not to play into it further. "I have neither seen nor heard from Lord Glenrick since Wednesday," she replied, then added, more slowly as the thought had not previously occurred to her, "Nor Frances, for that matter."

"Nor have I."

She tried not to allow that response please her too much. "Frances said something about an elderly great-aunt who was in failing health."

"Here in London?" His tone was skeptical.

"I don't know." Had Frances even said? She could not remember. Perhaps they *had* left for Scotland—but it seemed unlikely that Frances would make such a journey at the height of the season to attend the sickbed of a relative she had never before mentioned in all the years of their acquaintance... not to mention not leave any word for any of the Lady Patronesses.

"Hmm," the marquis said.

His steps slowed until they ceased altogether.

He was silent for so long, his brow creased, that after a long minute Annabel asked, "Are you well, sir?"

He started and resumed walking. "I beg your pardon. I am not being a very entertaining companion, which is most remiss of me after I basely extracted you from the bosom of your family in order to monopolize your attention."

She laughed. "You do talk the most complete nonsense. Was that something you learned at Eton, or is it a natural ability?"

"What nonsense? I am always quite serious, Fellbridge. I have every intention of monopolizing your attention whenever possible."

She stole a glance at him to try to gauge his expression, but his face was bland and unrevealing. What had got into him today? She was used to his teasing, but this was different. If anything, she would call it *flirting,* which left her feeling very off balance indeed.

Two months ago, she would have said that Lord Quinceton was the last man she would ever set up a flirtation with—in fact, she'd spoken those very words to Emily. And then he'd somehow insinuated himself into her life and thoughts till—till now she had to admit that she found his company. . . well, exhilarating. And perhaps more.

She took refuge in changing the subject. "Very well. If we are to talk nonsense, then what is this I am hearing about the Duke of Cumberland? My father was very full of it this morning, thanks to a waiter at Grillon's."

"You don't know?"

"I know only the smallest bit. I was otherwise occupied last week with the Ronderleys, if you recall."

"Yes, I suppose you were. There's not much to say; the duke is said to have been attacked by his valet, who then seems to have changed his mind and ended his own life instead. Is that what your father said?"

"More or less, with a little extra sordid speculation as to why such a thing had happened." She shook her head. "I pity the king. He's a good man, I think—why are most of his sons so prone to trouble and scandal? I am reminded of the fairy story where the bad fairy who wasn't invited to the christening comes anyway and curses the king's child—or children in this case—out of sheer spite. First there was that dreadful business last year with the Duke of York and his mistress that made him resign from the Army, and now this."

Again to her surprise, he didn't laugh. "I've thought that myself," he said slowly. "Not so much a bad fairy but something else—or perhaps I should say someone."

Annabel was not a Lady Patroness for nothing. Lord Quinceton did not miss much, as she'd learned to her occasional dismay. If *he* thought something peculiar was going on. . . "Whom do you suspect?" she asked sharply.

"Oh no you don't, Fellbridge. This investigation is not for you."

"But you think there is something worth investigating?"

"I don't know yet. I may be dragged into it

against my will—no," he said firmly, as she opened her mouth. "If there *is* anything going on, I do not wish to see you of all people mixed up in it."

It was on the tip of her tongue to ask why not her of all people, but his expression was so forbidding that she did not argue further. She would, however, report this conversation at tomorrow's meeting of the Lady Patronesses. In the meanwhile, they had reached the river's edge, and just now she wanted to put these discomfiting thoughts aside and simply enjoy the day and her sons' pleasure in it.

On the river, all the boats had been bedecked with flowers in honor of the king, and the boys wore the most outlandish collections of clothing they could manage by way of festive costume; even their hats were garlanded and beribboned. Will's boat was close enough to the bank that he saw Annabel waving and nearly dropped his oar waving back; a friendly cuff to the back of his shoulder from the older boy behind him just made him grin.

"I've not seen your sons before. They're ludicrously like their father," Lord Quinceton commented.

"Yes, aren't they?" Annabel replied. It felt decidedly odd to be discussing Freddy with him.

"I suspect, however, that they have their mother's brains. Your late husband may have been the best of good fellows, but he could be thick as a plank at times, regrettably."

Annabel glanced up at him, but there was no ironical quirk to his expression. How was she supposed to respond to such a statement, especially as she was in complete accord with it? "His intentions were good," was all she could think of to say.

"You are kind enough to not speak ill of the dead. I have fewer such compunctions. I don't know that I can ever forgive him—" He stopped speaking, instead staring into the distance across the river, his lips compressed.

Annabel blinked at the bitterness in his voice. Forgive what? What could Freddy have ever done to him? She waited for him to finish, but he remained unwontedly silent, so she sighed and tried to think of something else to say. "I do hope the boys will be careful. Those boats look so fragile."

"The river should be past its spring spate by now," Lord Quinceton said in a much more normal tone. "Nothing to be concerned about." He smiled reminiscently. "I remember being out in one when it wasn't. Fortunately, my mother was not there to see me."

"Why am I not surprised to learn that you were an incorrigible child?"

"I beg your pardon, madam, but I was no such thing. In that particular instance, in fact, I was victim rather than perpetrator—and a fortunate one. The river was in a forgiving mood that day, and we made it to shore unharmed if in a damper condition than when we were launched by a group of fourth form boys who thought it would be a capital joke to send a group of first years out without oars."

"Good heavens. I hope that sort of behavior is no longer permitted." Annabel shuddered as she gazed out at the river. Although Will and Martin might not mind such japes—they were, in that respect, very much their father's sons—*she* certainly found them alarming. She looked again at Will's boat and frowned; was the water flowing a little faster than it had been moments before? But no, that could not be.

"It wasn't permitted then, either. If it makes you feel better, I am under the impression that that sort of tomfoolery has lessened somewhat since my day."

"I should hope so! Well, Gus, and how are you?" she said kindly as Augustus Blackburn hurried over to them, his eyes fastened on her worshipfully.

"I'm very well, Lady Fellbridge." He bowed. "Is Martin with you?"

"I'm afraid Martin decided to go to the picnic field in my carriage."

"Oh." His face fell, and she wondered if he and the boys had indeed had a falling out. Was that why Martin had insisted on leaving without him? But Gus straightened his shoulders and said, "Never mind. I ought to get started." He started to turn away, then hesitated. "Will—will you be there, ma'am?"

"Yes, Gus, and I hope you will join our picnic. Will and Martin's grandparents are here as well."

"Oh, thank you!" For a moment she thought he would fling his arms around her. Poor creature, he probably did not receive many hugs. Then he bowed again, grinning happily, and joined the surge of boys streaming toward the river path.

"A friend, I take it?" Lord Quinceton said.

"My sons' friend, Gus Blackburn." She didn't elaborate, hoping he would not recall Maria's rashly blurted explanation about Gus's being the culprit in the voucher-forging incident several weeks ago. The boy had already grown since April; Annabel remembered their conversation about affording new coats and was glad that for a few years at least his basic wants would be met. Perhaps his father could be recalled to his responsibilities before the money Gus had accumulated ran out.

"Ah. So that's Master Blackburn," Lord Quinceton said. "I trust the child has avoided further criminal activity?"

Drat it, he remembered. "He didn't commit a crime. Well, not an actionable one anyway," she amended. "And what he did was understandable under the circumstances."

Just then, a shouted "Oy!" made her look up—and gasp. The boats already on the river (some were still drawn up to the bank awaiting guest passengers) were rocking and heaving as if under a heavy swell. Boys frantically worked their oars, trying to keep the narrow craft from capsizing in the sudden waves rolling down the river.

"William!" She pulled away from Lord Quinceton. What had happened to roil the river so suddenly? A moment ago, it had been calm and sparkling gently in the sun—

A hand closed on her shoulder, halting her. "Be still, Fellbridge," Lord Quinceton said in her ear.

"My son is out there!"

"And just what do you think you can do for him?"

Her breath caught in her throat. Oh, a pox on him for being right!

But as she watched, straining despite herself against Lord Quinceton's iron grip on her arm, the river quickly subsided, looking once more like a river and not like the Channel in a tempest, and the boats stopped threatening to capsize. She anxiously scanned them until she spotted Will, still safely seated if a little scared looking. "I thought you said the river was past its spring spate?" she said, her voice shaky.

Lord Quinceton released her arm. He was watching the surface of the river closely. "It is. What did you see?"

"Wasn't it obvious?"

"I have a reason for asking. Be precise, please."

She restrained an impulse to argue and reviewed the images in her mind. "I. . . don't know. It—it's foolish, but. . . it looked almost as if the surface of the water was trying to shake the boats off as a horse does a fly. But that's—" She shook her head. "What did *you* see?"

He was still watching the river. "More or less what you did."

"I didn't know rivers did that sort of thing."

"They don't, usually."

"Then what—"

"I don't know. Unless. . ." A frown drew his brows down. "No. They couldn't have forgotten," he muttered.

"Who?" Again, perhaps it was being a Lady Patroness, but she had the distinct impression that there was something odd going on here. . . and that he knew something about it. "Forgotten what?"

He stared out at the river for a moment longer, then seemed to come to a decision. "Are you up to a brisk walk?"

"What, immediately? Can't we watch the start of the procession?"

"I think it would be best if we leave now, so that we may keep the boats in view."

Ah. So there *was* something going on. She looked again at the boats full of laughing boys, already recovered from their scare a moment before. "I am, if you will tell me what is concerning you about the river."

He smiled as he led her toward the path Gus had taken. "But my dear Fellbridge, you have not been very forthcoming when I have asked similar questions recently."

"I—I have not always been at liberty to answer questions that concern other people's affairs."

He looked down at her and raised an eyebrow. "Nor am I."

She took a breath. "Lord Quinceton, I must ask you to tell me if there something amiss with the river. If there is, I think I deserve to know about it. My elder son is in a boat upon it as we speak."

They had overtaken a rowdy knot of fifth formers on the path, a couple of them on what looked like borrowed cart-horses. The marquis steered them past the boisterous, incongruously flower-bedecked group without speaking. When they were no longer in earshot, he said quietly, "I fear that there's something amiss with the Tamesian Potamides."

"The *what*?"

"Tamesian Potamides." He looked at her sideways. "Also known as the river nymphs of the Thames."

Annabel was careful not to allow her expression to change. *River nymphs?* Was he hoaxing her?

But no: she had always been truthful with him, even if she hadn't always been forthcoming with *all* of the truth. She somehow knew that he was according her the same courtesy. And if he believed—no, if he knew that there were river nymphs in the Thames, it would explain why he'd been so accepting of the book demons and Sirens she'd discussed with him. *How* he knew about these river nymphs—now *that* would be an interesting topic for discussion.

"I was not aware that the Thames had resident nymphs," she said—remarkably calmly, she thought.

"All of Britain's rivers have them. They only become of concern when the river is navigable. There is a crown officer whose duty it is to"—he paused—"to maintain cordial relations with the inhabitants of rivers upon which human commerce takes place, most specifically the Thames. If the Thames nymphs are happy, it seems their sisters in other rivers are as well. With the occasional exception, of course."

"Really? Which officer is that?" She examined

him carefully; from the lack of a certain look in his eye, she was reasonably certain he was not hoaxing her. Did the Lady Patronesses know about this? There were a number of crown officials whose duties and titles went back hundreds of years, the reasons for their existence now almost lost in history. Perhaps this was one of those.

"It's not one you'll have heard of. The royal office of the King's Maintenancer of the Tamesian Potamides is not frequently discussed, for obvious reasons."

The King's—heavens, that was a mouthful. "How do you know about it, then?"

"My grandfather held it under George II. It's not a sinecure as are some of the other old offices. The King's Maintenancer is an envoy. He is supposed to meet with the Thames nymphs sometime in early spring and negotiate an annual tribute to avert excessive spring flooding and guarantee human safety on the rivers for the year. Within reason, of course. If some drunken lout falls off a bridge on his way home from the pub and drowns, that's his affair. But the nymphs promise not to prey on humans who happen to be on or near a river, minding their own business." His eyes grew distant. "Grandfather took me to a meeting with them on one occasion when I was a boy."

Annabel tried not to think of nymphs preying on people on the river. "That must have been interesting."

"Quite, as they took a fancy to me and wanted to keep me as part of the annual settlement that year."

They were passing another group of boys at that moment, or Annabel would have demanded a further account of that meeting. But just now there were more immediate matters to discuss. "And you think that what the river did just now is a sign that something is upsetting the river nymphs?"

"I don't know. I worry that it might be."

"Might the present, er, Maintenancer not be fulfilling his office properly? Who is he, anyway? Or are you allowed to know?"

"The House of Lords is aware of the King's Maintenancer and what he does, since he's traditionally drawn from our ranks. The present incumbent is Lord Rossing."

Rossing... when had she run across that name recently? Then she remembered. "I saw him not so long ago—at the Summer Exhibition with Lord Glenrick." And he'd not looked pleased at her and Eliza's interruption of their *tête-à-tête*. "What can be done if he's not properly fulfilling his duties?"

"I don't know. It's never happened before." His voice had gone oddly flat.

"Why should a crown officer not do his job, anyway?"

Lord Quinceton did not reply for a long moment. At last he said, "That is a very good question."

They hurried along the path, overtaking several groups of boys and other holiday makers, including her parents. Approaching them from behind, Annabel was struck by how content they looked. Mama's face, just visible past the edge of her parasol as she turned her head to say something to Papa, wore a sunny smile; Papa's responding laugh as he patted her hand resting on his arm was warm and happy. It had always been so between them, no matter how much Papa pretended to bluster and Mama to tease him in return, and below it was a bedrock of affection and devotion that Annabel couldn't help envying. Perhaps it was because they were closer in age than she and Freddy had been and had more in common. . . or perhaps it was simply that Freddy had not wanted such a relationship with her.

She touched Papa's sleeve as she and Lord Quinceton drew even with them. "Dawdlers," she said, wrinkling her nose at him.

"*Slow and steady wins the race*, minx," he said cheerfully.

"*The race is to the swift,*" Mama intoned.

Papa frowned. "I don't think that's how that one originally goes, m'dear, although I can't help suspecting you've got the right end of it. Do you see how it goes with me, sir?" he said to Lord Quinceton. "I am beleaguered from all sides. Beleaguered, I say!"

Lord Quinceton inclined his head. "I have heard it said, sir, that what is sauce for the goose is sauce for the gander."

Annabel was startled into laughing out loud. "Oh, Papa, he has you there!"

"Hmmph. So much for masculine unity in the face of feminine onslaught," Papa replied in a grumpy tone, but his eyes were twinkling. "Why are you two in such a hurry?" he added as Lord Quinceton led her past them.

"Oh—we, er, need to keep Martin from eating

all the food before we get there. We'll see you shortly," Annabel called over her shoulder.

"Leave them be, George," Mama said. "Four would definitely be a crowd."

"Oh ho! Sits the wind in that corner?" Papa said, and then they were too far behind for any further conversation to be heard, thank heavens. Oh, Mama—was she so eager to see her younger daughter remarried that she saw potential suitors in every man Annabel chanced to speak with? If only she could convince herself that Lord Quinceton had not heard that bit of conversation. . . but she knew too well how observant he was—

A glance to the side quickly banished any thoughts of Mama and suitors: the river had grown darker, the water grayer and more turbulent even in the golden light of late afternoon. "Look," she said quietly to Lord Quinceton.

He was already looking. "Damnation. We should have taken my curricle after all."

Annabel did not care for the sound of that in the least. "Would it not be better to wait for the boats to come into view? At least we could watch for them and help in case the nymphs—in case something happens."

"And help how, with no boat of our own? Can you swim, Fellbridge?"

"I wish I could!"

He smiled. "Perhaps I shall teach you one day. But in the meanwhile, I think it behooves us to hurry to the field. If there is to be a contretemps with the Potamides over their missing tribute, I expect they'll want to hold it where it will likely have the largest audience." His step quickened; Annabel grimly clung to his arm and resolved to keep up with him if it killed her.

She had not had time to become more than a little out of breath when the sound of thudding hooves could be heard from behind them. To her surprise, rather than withdrawing to the side to allow the approaching horsemen to pass, Lord Quinceton turned and stood firm in the middle of the path.

A pair of horses so large and broad that their usual occupation must have involved drawing a plow soon cantered into view, their gait majestic if no faster than a trot would have been in a lesser beast. One of their riders, a husky Eton sixth-former, shouted "Whoa, then," when he saw them standing in the path, and drew rein.

"I say," his red-haired companion began, as his lumbering steed finally halted just a few feet away. "It's really rather bad form to be blocking the path in such a fashion."

"My apologies for troubling you, but I should be greatly obliged if you would lend me your horse," Lord Quinceton replied calmly.

"What?" The boy goggled at him.

"Your horse. It is vital that I get to the field without delay. Quite possibly a matter of life and death."

Annabel gasped.

The red-haired boy sneered. "Oh, really? And why, precisely, should I believe that? What do you think this is, Montem—only you're demanding people's cattle instead of their money?"

"No. I always thought Montem was a silly custom."

But the husky boy prodded his friend. "The lady seems to think it's serious," he said, gesturing at Annabel. "If I may ask, sir, who are you, and what guarantee can you give us that you won't, er, steal our horses? They're not ours, you see, and perhaps we were a trifle out-of-hand to have borrowed them without the farmer saying in so many words that we could—"

Lord Quinceton reached into a pocket, then handed his card up to the boy. "I have no intention of making off with your horse. You shall ride with me and reclaim it at the field as soon as we both arrive there."

The boy looked at the card and whistled. "Beg pardon, my lord. If it's as you say—you can take Diablo here, and I'll go with Gerrold. There's no saddle, I'm afraid." He slid off the horse—it was a long way down—adjusted the blanket, and handed over the reins. "Here, I'll give you a leg up."

"A plow horse named Diablo. Why am I not surprised?" Lord Quinceton said, making use of the boy's offered hands as a step and heaving himself astride the enormous animal. Diablo turned its head and surveyed them with an air of gentle surprise. "What's his friend's name?"

"Lucifer. The farmer has a sense of humor." The boy grinned.

"See here, Watts!" The red-haired boy's complexion was fast rivaling his locks in hue. "You can't just hand over one of our—"

"Stow it, Gerrold. If it would help, sir, we can

ride ahead and clear the path for you—although how I'll get up on Lucifer without a mounting block is an interesting ques—"

"Excuse me." Annabel stepped forward.

"Er, ma'am?" The husky boy started, as if he'd forgotten she was there.

"Lord Quinceton, do you actually intend to leave me here while you ride off to rescue *my* son?" Annabel demanded.

Lord Quinceton looked down at her, one eyebrow raised. "Can't stand to miss the action, Fellbridge?"

"Why, you—you—"

"Mr. Watts, would you be so kind as to assist Lady Fellbridge? Between us we can probably hoist her up onto this block of marble you call a horse."

Annabel suddenly remembered that a bronze muslin walking dress and half-boots were not appropriate riding attire, but it was too late to change her mind: young Watts, blushing violently, mumbled, "If you'll forgive me, ma'am," and caught her round the waist. She gamely jumped to add her own momentum to his lifting and felt Lord Quinceton's hands catch her up under the arms from behind at the same time—and suddenly she was seated sideways on Diablo's broad back. The small crowd of spectators who had come up behind them and gathered on the path to watch their doings cheered.

"You'll have to hold on to me, Fellbridge," Lord Quinceton said, glancing back at her over his shoulder. "I don't intend to go at a sedate walk."

Annabel thought of the horse's lumbering

canter. Why had she thought this would be a good idea? It was too late to rethink her actions, however, so she slid her arms awkwardly around his middle. "What is the thing that boy said?" she asked. "Mountain, I think?"

"Montem. It's a quaint Eton custom that would get anyone else hanged for highway robbery. The boys have *carte blanche* on Montem Day—it's only done once every three years, now—to stop carriages on the Bath road and demand a fee for continued passage."

Good heavens! "Why, whatever for?"

"For the benefit of the Senior Colleger moving on to Cambridge, to help with expenses."

"What an odd custom."

She felt him shrug. "Eton has a lot of those. It started out as some sort of initiation rite for new boys, I believe. Lord knows why it changed."

"Hi, are we off?" Watts had managed to scramble up behind Gerrold on Lucifer, neither of whom seemed sanguine about the idea. "Tally ho and all that!"

Lucifer shook his head as if exasperated and commenced an amble, then broke into a thunderous trot at the boys' urging. "We'll clear the path, sir," Watts called back to them. "See you soon!"

Diablo, seeing his companion dashing off—relatively speaking—into parts unknown, followed suit, and Annabel's tentative hold on Lord Quinceton quickly tightened lest she be tossed ignominiously from her precarious sideways perch.

For some minutes she did nothing but hang

on. But as she eventually grew used to their movement down the narrow river path, she was able to consider her position in relation to Lord Quinceton. It was an odd sensation to have her arms around him; she had embraced no other man to whom she was not closely related but Freddy. The difference between them was a revelation: Freddy had been more than a little podgy around the middle—a great deal more, in fact—while Lord Quinceton was all strength, with no softness or superfluous flesh. Yet there was a suppleness to him as well that was fascinating—she could feel it as he moved in response to the horse's gait. The result of all the time he reportedly spent fencing at Angelo's, perhaps? Why had no one told her that embracing a man could be such a delicious experience, physically speaking?

She rested her cheek against his back and nestled closer for several more minutes, the better to feel him. . . then jerked her head upright again in mortification. What was she doing? Would he think she was *hugging* him, rather than just hanging on for dear life?

"Are you still in one piece, Fellbridge?"

"I'm quite well, thank you."

"Do be careful. It would be most inconvenient to have you fall off."

She snorted. "I would be devastated to inconvenience you, my lord."

"Would you? I shall have to remember that." There was a smile in his voice.

"It would serve you right if I squeezed so firmly that you couldn't breathe!"

"A challenge! Do your worst, madam."

"Very well, I will!" She pressed more firmly against his back, stretched her arms as far as they would go around him, and squeezed with all her might.

He laughed. "Is that the best you can do? Behold, I still breathe."

"It's not a fair contest! I can't get a proper grip on you, sitting sideways in this fashion."

"Hmm, true. Very well; when we have restored Diablo to his erstwhile guardians, you shall try again to squeeze the breath from me from whatever vantage point you please."

Annabel started to answer, but a recollection of what such a contest might involve sent a flood of color into her face. "You are quite ridiculous, sir. That is not necessary."

"Coward," he said amiably. "The offer stands. Ah, I believe we're nearly there."

## Chapter Three

"Here we are!" Watts called back to them a moment later, unconsciously echoing Lord Quinceton.

"Here" was another green field overlooking the river, a-bask in the golden sun of late afternoon. Unlike the Brocas, this field had sprouted little clusters of folding chairs and tables where picnics had been set up by bored-looking footmen; a few early spectators had already broken out the champagne and sandwiches. On the far side of the grassy expanse, a crowd of boys clustered around something that she couldn't quite see. And as for the river, which Annabel had been facing away from on their ride on Diablo. . . it still flowed placidly by, empty of boats. But there was a sense of stirring below its surface, as if the current were running more swiftly than usual.

Watts and Gerrold had already dismounted,

and Watts came hurrying to them. "Help you down, ma'am?" he asked.

With his assistance, Annabel slid off Diablo's broad back. For a moment she missed the security of the sensation of Lord Quinceton's body against hers—but that was foolishness. And anyway, she should be thinking of Will and the river nymphs, not Lord Quinceton's body.

"All right, Fellbridge?" Lord Quinceton asked her, sliding off the horse in turn.

"Very well, thank you." Well, mostly; whilst she had survived the ride unscathed, her dress had not. Diablo had evidently not had a bath in the recent past. Oh dear, Winters would scold!

He nodded, handed the reins to Watts with a curt "thank you," and strode toward the river.

"Ma'am, if I may. . ." Watts began shyly. "Er, what was the matter of life and death?"

"I expect you'll know shortly," Annabel said. The river was growing darker even as they spoke, although no boats were yet in sight.

Watts followed her glance, and his eyes widened. "Good Lord! What's up with that? Say, Gerrold! Gerrold! Look!" He hurried toward his friend, towing Diablo behind him like an equine barge.

Annabel began to follow Lord Quinceton to the river's edge, but a chance glance at the crowd of boys across the field halted her: a momentary thinning revealed a glimpse of a table and a flaming torch.

"Martin?" she breathed. It had to be—but what had the boy been up to now? Was this the—the whatever-it-was that he had planned in honor of the king's birthday? Somehow he'd never told her precisely what it was he intended. . .

With one more glance at Lord Quinceton and the still boat-free river, she began to make her way to the crowd of boys. With any luck she could find out what Martin was up to before she needed to be on hand to help Will—if she could.

As she approached the crowd, she caught more glimpses of the planks atop the trestles that Martin had loaded into her carriage. The makeshift tables were covered with something; now and again she saw a basket, a platter, a bowl—

The table was groaning with food. Dodging and weaving between happily munching boys, Annabel saw platters of sandwiches of all descriptions, from dainty watercress to hearty spiced ham; piles of Scotch eggs in their golden breadcrumb coats; turnovers and pasties in profusion; every conceivable kind of biscuit—and cakes, dozens of cakes, including some iced a delicate pink that looked very familiar. . . as did the platter on which they sat—

And behind the table stood Martin, flanked by two of his friends. The three of them were accepting coins from the crowd and making change with expert speed. Good heavens, they were *selling* all this food—some of which had come from the picnic hampers she and Mama had brought. But where had the rest of it come from? And just why was Martin selling it?

"Martin Chalfont!" she called, in a voice she knew her son would hear—and understand.

The crowd of boys froze and fell silent. Evidently they understood that tone as well.

Martin's eyes grew very large—and then his face melted into a parent-cajoling smile that she was far too familiar with. She finished pushing through the crowd and came to a halt in front of him.

"I do believe an explanation is in order," she said—which she thought showed almost Olympian restraint.

Martin didn't blink. Freddy, who'd been a dreadful card player, would have been proud. "Mother! What a—a surprise! I didn't expect to see you so soon."

"Clearly not." She surveyed the table. "I think that you and I must have a talk."

"Er, can't it wait for a bit? I'm monstrous busy—"

"*Now*," Annabel said, stepping sideways around the table and firmly grasping her son by the elbow.

"See to the table, men!" Martin called over his shoulder as she propelled him some distance from the crowd. When they were mostly out of hearing distance, she fixed him with a stern look.

"Now, Martin, what is going on here? Is this why you were so anxious for your grandmother and me to bring large picnics? So you could sell it to the other boys?"

Martin fixed his guileless blue eyes on hers. "Not. . . entirely. And it wasn't just you and Gran—I swear!"

"I had guessed that, looking at that table."

"All our friends agreed to help. We've got at least a dozen hampers!" He looked up at her, clearly expecting praise.

He didn't get it. "Has it not occurred to you that the providers of those hampers might be just a little put out when they find their picnics have been sold to a horde of hungry boys? Martin, you've stolen their food from them—and worse, are selling their belongings for profit—"

"Not for *profit*, Mama!" he interjected, all outraged dignity.

"No? Then what is it for?"

He looked down at his feet. "For Gus."

"For. . . Gus?" Had she heard him correctly? "But why?"

Martin straightened his shoulders and left off looking at his feet. There was no cajolery in his expression now. "Gus told us about what he did with your Almack's vouchers when he came home with us, and how bad he felt that he'd got you in trouble with the other ladies. He said he couldn't keep that money he'd made because it was wrongfully acquired—" He broke off and asked, "Did he *really* make seven hundred guineas?"

"Yes, he did."

"By Jove!" He gave an admiring whistle. "Our Gus did that?"

"Martin, what did Gus do with the money?" Annabel demanded.

"Oh, he sent it to the Exploration Society or someplace like that." He shrugged. "He said that giving it to a worthy cause was the best thing he could do to make up for what he did."

Tears started in Annabel's eyes. Oh, the gallant child!

But Martin hadn't finished. "We knew he was back in the suds as far as paying his fees here. So we decided to do something to help him, and got this brilliant idea. *I* thought of it," he added modestly. "It's a sort of Montem—it's a special Eton thing—"

"I know what Montem is."

"You do?" Martin regarded her equal amounts of respect and dismay. "But you're a—a *mother*. You're not supposed to know that sort of thing!"

"You'd be surprised, dear." She didn't think it necessary to add that she'd just come by the knowledge a half-hour ago. "Go on."

"Well, we thought we'd have our own Montem to raise money for Gus. Sort of," he added, after a moment's thought. "It's not exactly the same—"

A shout from the direction of the river, followed by several more exclamations and cries of distress, reminded Annabel that the child before her was not the only one of her sons in trouble that afternoon. Her throat tightened. Where was Lord Quinceton? And where was Will? Had the boats begun to arrive. . . along with angry river nymphs? She turned to scan the riverbank, but it was crowded with arriving spectators, all staring intently at the river. What was happening down there?

"What was that?" Martin followed her gaze. "Are the boats here? Are they having a bumping-race? Brilliant!" He started for the river.

Annabel caught him by the back of his jacket. "I don't know what is happening, but you're staying here. I'm not done with you—or rather, your grandfather won't be, when he finds his picnic has been eaten from under him."

For the first time, Martin looked apprehensive. "Er, I could set aside a plate or two. . ."

"That might help," Annabel said over her shoulder. She gave him a little push toward his table and turned back to the river. Bother it, she should have known Martin was up to something back at the Brocas—but how could she be angry with him for wanting to help his friend? Him and Will—oh, why had she not insisted Will leave his boat when that first wave had nearly swamped it?

She hadn't gone more than a few steps before she heard someone call, "Annabel! There you are!" Maria Sefton was picking her way across the field toward her.

"Maria!" She'd forgotten that the Seftons were here today. Oh, thank goodness there was another Lady Patroness on hand! Perhaps Maria spoke whatever language the nymphs did and could plead with them not to hurt the boys in the boats.

Maria grasped her arm as they met. "I do wish fields didn't have to be so tussocky. It's quite impossible to walk across one without turning an ankle. Annabel, I'm afraid we have a rather unpleasant mess to deal with—"

"The river nymphs—I know."

Maria looked surprised. "You do?"

"Well, it's what Lord Quinceton thinks is going on. He suspects they've not received their tribute this spring and are showing their anger."

"Ah." Maria nodded. "I should have remembered he would know about them. What I wish to know is *why* they haven't received it, if that is indeed what is wrong. We shall certainly have to bring this up at tomorrow's meeting. Where is Quin, anyway?"

"By the river, last I saw him." Annabel took Maria's arm and started to steer her toward the riverbank. She spotted Lord Quinceton amid a crowd close to the water's edge, with young Messrs. Watts and Gerrold beside him, looking excited.

"I wondered what had become of you," he said as Annabel finished dodging and weaving through the crowd and reached his side. "Lady Sefton," he added, nodding to Maria.

"My other son required my attention. It seems he's commandeered half the picnics in the field and is selling them off to hungry schoolboys. No wonder he wanted to be certain that I brought plenty of his favorite iced cakes." She was amazed at how even her voice was.

"Enterprising fellow." He smiled, but his gaze never left the river.

Annabel took in the roiling surface of the quick-flowing water and shivered. "I heard a shout a few minutes ago. . . ?"

"Just a brief water-spout. For our entertainment, I suspect. Don't worry, the boats aren't here yet, although I suspect they soon will be."

"Can't we do something before that?" Two enormous waves impossibly approached each other from opposite directions and collided as if they were adversarial mountains; Annabel winced at the spray that spumed twenty feet in the air.

"Until the authors of this commotion choose

to present themselves, I can't think of anything."

"Do you know what's causing this, sir?" Watts said. "I've never seen the river—er—behave in this manner."

"No, you wouldn't have," Lord Quinceton said absently. "Ah—is that—?"

The rest of his words were drowned in a collective rumble from the crowd around them as the first of the boats came gliding into view—although gliding was perhaps not the most apt description of its action. The surface of the Thames looked positively oceanic now, and the bow of the boat pitched up and down as the boys tried to maintain the rhythm of their strokes in the face of the waves. A second boat followed them closely, then a third and a fourth, and more.

As their boats approached the field, the rowers in each stopped rowing, lifted their oars from the water, and raised them till they were vertical, perpendicular to the water—or at least as vertical as they could manage under the circumstances.

"Good God," Watts gasped. "They're not going to attempt the salute, are they?"

"They'll be over the side in no time. We'll be fishing bodies out of the river till Election Day!" Gerrold answered with ghoulish glee.

"What salute?" Annabel demanded.

"It's what they do at the end of the procession—all the boys raise their oars and stand up in their boats to salute the king," Watts explained. "But not today—surely not when the river's in such a state—"

The boys in the first boat began, as one, to stand. It would have been an impressive sight—the straight young forms, the small forest of oars—but a malevolently-aimed wave did just as Gerrold predicted and upset their boat. Boys and oars were launched into the angry waters amid a great, oddly greenish fountain of spray.

Annabel cried out. She was not alone; the spectators lining the banks were in an uproar, but their shouts were not louder than the boys' own cries of distress.

"Come on, Gerrold!" Watts shouted, stripping off his jacket and kicking off his shoes before diving for the river. At least a dozen older boys did the same, while others waded in more slowly to form human chains reaching out to the middle of the river. Then another boat went over, and another—and to her horror, Annabel realized that the third boat contained her son.

"Will!" she cried.

"Where?" Lord Quinceton asked sharply.

All she could do was mutely point toward the river; all the breath seemed to have been sucked from her chest.

Watts and Gerrold and the boys who could swim had almost reached the floundering occupants of the first boat, half of whom had managed to catch hold of the hull of their overturned craft. But now other figures were visible in the water with them—figures almost but not quite human in shape, with long arms and disproportionately short legs ending in flat, elongated feet that could be seen as they scythed through the water. And most inhuman in color; their skin was a greenish light brown, and their trailing hair very definitely green. Annabel watched, horrified, as they converged on the next arriving boat and neatly tipped it over. Others of the creatures were swimming toward the boys clinging to their boats, their long, dark eyes narrowed with angry intent.

"Well, that more or less answers our questions." Maria's voice was hollow.

Annabel leaned closer to her. "What can we do?" she whispered urgently. "That is—you and I?"

Maria shook her head. "I don't know. I'm of no help here; I've no idea what language they speak. Is there anything you could do with your shadows?"

Annabel thought furiously. Covering this stretch of the river with shadow wouldn't accomplish anything more than to make it difficult to see what was happening and inspire panic. Nor would it hamper the angry nymphs at all—they would simply stay under water. She could make ropes of shadow to help the rescuers reach the boys, but unless she kept hold of each one, they would quickly dissolve in the golden sunlight slanting down on the river.

"No," she said, and heard her voice catch on a sob. "There's nothing we can do."

The nymphs had almost reached the first boat. One of them rose up in the water and shouted, "If we don't get our due, then we'll have to take you! A good dinner you'll make us all!" A boy shrieked and almost lost his grip on the overturned hull; something appeared to be tugging on his legs beneath the roiling surface of the water.

Annabel's knees all at once no longer seemed capable of supporting her weight. Will! Oh God, her poor darling boy!

But a hand, warm and firm, grasped her arm, keeping her from collapsing. "Bear up, Fellbridge!" Lord Quinceton said. "The boys aren't being hurt—the nymphs are just trying to frighten them. See? None have gone under."

"They're succeeding remarkably well at frightening me!" she managed to mutter, and willed herself to remain standing until her legs capitulated and agreed to behave themselves. Was that Will there, near that boat? So much obscured her view—floundering boys, dropped oars, and the angry gray-green of the water itself. "If they are hungry, we could have invited them to our picnic—except Martin has likely sold off all the iced cakes and sandwiches—"

Lord Quinceton's hand on her arm tightened. "That's it!"

"What?"

He released her arm and grabbed her hand. "Come on. It's worth a try."

"What is?" she demanded, then squeaked in surprise as he started to hurry away, still gripping her hand.

"Where are you going?" Maria called after them.

"To do something about this," Lord Quinceton replied over his shoulder as he threaded a path through the crowd. "Where is your son and his table?" he said more quietly to Annabel.

"Over there, at the far side of the field. Near

the trees." Annabel was getting a stitch in her side, her hat felt in imminent danger of flying off her head, and Maria's hated tussocks seemed to be catching at her toes. "What—are you going—to do?" she gasped.

"Precisely what you said. Invite the nymphs to our picnic."

It was on the tip of her tongue to accuse him of lunacy, but she refrained. "Do you really—think that will work?"

"It will be a sign of respect. Right now I suspect it's mostly the Potamides' pride that's been hurt. If we can soothe that now, it will give us time to rescue the boys and negotiate their proper tribute—and find out why they haven't already received it," he added grimly.

Just before Annabel's wind completely gave out, they arrived at Martin's table. The crowd around it had thinned somewhat; many boys had been drawn away by the commotion on the water, but a dozen or so still milled around. They drew back as she and Lord Quinceton strode into their midst.

"Listen here, dry bobs!" Lord Quinceton shouted. Annabel wondered how he had any breath left to do so. "Where's Martin Chalfont!"

"Here, sir." Behind the table, which still held a bounteous number of cakes, tarts, and sandwiches, Martin drew himself straight. But Annabel could see the apprehension in his eyes as he looked at Lord Quinceton, who suddenly appeared very tall and authoritative indeed.

"We need this food down at the river. There's

a problem there, and this might solve it. You—all of you"—he waved a hand at the nearest boys—"grab a plate and follow me."

"Hey!" Martin ran around the side of the table, waving his arms. "You can't do that! We're raising money for Gus! They'll kick him out if he can't pay his fees!"

"Would you rather raise money for Gus or save your brother's life?" Lord Quinceton asked. "Don't worry about Master Blackburn. He has already been provided for. Now help us carry this down to the water."

"My brother?" Martin gulped and looked scared. "What's wrong with Will?"

"Nothing for now, but I can't promise it will remain that way unless we hurry." He swept them all with a stern look. "I'm relying on your assistance. Now go!"

He'd hit just the right note; Martin's fear turned to determination. "Come on then, men!" He grabbed a platter.

Annabel picked up a plate of sandwiches. "Master Blackburn has been *what*?" she said to Lord Quinceton. How did he know anything about Gus?

He didn't reply but seized a platter of her iced cakes and turned toward the river. She and Martin and the rest of the boys fell into place behind him.

"Is Will hurt?" Martin asked in a small voice.

"No, of *course* not," Annabel said, as firmly as she could.

"But your friend said—"

"Will is not hurt," she repeated. "But he is in

trouble, as are all the other boys who were on boats."

"What will the food do to help them?"

Annabel hesitated. "It's. . . difficult to explain. Just do what Lord Quinceton says when we get to the river. Promise?"

He nodded vigorously, but a small sigh escaped him. "And we were going on dreadfully well, too. I'll bet we would have sold everything by the time we needed to go back to the Brocas for the fireworks."

At the river's edge, pandemonium reigned. A group of sodden boys, rescued by the swimmers, huddled on the bank; alas, Will was not among their number. Rescuers still braved the seething river and the nymphs, dragging boys to shore, but the waters were almost too turbulent for them to risk further forays. The spectators shouted and waved, boys ran about doing the same, and the various horses (and a cow or two) borrowed for the occasion milled skittishly about the field, forgotten by their riders in the excitement.

Lord Quinceton was standing by the water's edge, his feet bare, being helped out of his coat by a sodden Watts. A pair of wide-eyed younger boys looked on, holding his hat and the platter of cakes.

"There you are, Fellbridge," he said conversationally as she came up to him. "Would you be so good as to stand guard over my boots for a quarter-hour?"

"Your *what*?" Annabel handed her plate of sandwiches to Martin. "Good heavens, you aren't planning to *swim* out to the nymphs, are you?"

"I rather hope it doesn't come to that, but I shall have to wade out some ways, I expect, if I'm going to be able to speak with them. I'm afraid I must impose upon you to take charge of my hat and coat as well."

"Are you quite certain about this, sir?" Watts asked, trying not to drip on her as he handed Annabel the coat. "I can swim out there again if you need me to."

"Thank you, but I'm quite certain." Lord Quinceton untied his cravat, gave it to Annabel, and began to unbutton his waistcoat.

"But what are you going to *do*?"

"Not a great deal. My intention is to walk out no farther than I need to in order to speak with the nymphs and offer them something to eat."

"Something to eat?" Watts looked astonished.

Lord Quinceton smiled. "They have a tremendous appetite for sweets. I hope that a few plates of cakes and biscuits will distract them from harassing the boys and allow us to get them all safely ashore."

"Will you rescue my brother, sir?" Martin was pale, gazing out at the shrieking boys clinging to their boats.

Lord Quinceton shrugged out of his waistcoat and handed it to Annabel. "I will do my best to make sure *all* the boys are safe," he said seriously. "But if the opportunity arises, I shall certainly do whatever is in my power for your brother."

Martin nodded.

Annabel took the waistcoat. His clothes were warm in her arms, and she resisted the urge to hug them to her chest for reassurance. "Be careful, Quin," she said quietly.

He glanced at her from where he stood ankle-deep in the water, a slight smile quirking the corners of his mouth. "I will." Then he took the plate of Martin's favorite iced cakes—Martin watched them go with a regretful little sigh—and walked slowly into the Thames.

## Chapter Four

Annabel scarcely dared breathe as Lord Quinceton waded deeper into the turbulent water, pausing now and then to steady his footing.

"If he slips, ma'am, I'll be out there in a trice," Watts assured her.

She forced her grip on Lord Quinceton's clothing in her arms to relax. "I don't expect that he will."

"No, I don't either." Watts hesitated, then blurted, "Does he really believe that giving those creatures *cakes* will stop them?"

"He wouldn't be doing this if he didn't." The water was to his chest, and he was now carrying the platter of Mrs. Dailey's cakes over his head. She was relieved to see him halt and steady himself before opening his mouth.

"Potamides of the Thames, I bear you greetings!" he shouted.

For a moment, nothing changed: the boys'

shrieks still mixed with the howls and laughter of the nymphs swimming wildly about them while the thrashing snake that was the river continued to roil in its channel.

Suddenly a head—no, two heads, broke the surface a few yards from Lord Quinceton. They regarded him in silence, circling him as if examining a sculpture in an exhibition. He bore their scrutiny calmly. Then one of them rose up in the water—how was she able to do that?—and gave forth a string of strange, liquid-sounding syllables in a voice that somehow managed to be heard over the general cacophony. The other nymphs fell silent, and even the boys' cries grew quieter.

The nymph who'd silenced the rest with her call circled Lord Quinceton again. "I have seen you before," she said, halting in front of him. Even from shore Annabel could see that, whilst her face had two eyes, a nose of sorts, and a mouth, it was not human. "Many years ago."

Lord Quinceton somehow managed to bow while still holding the tray over his head. "My grandfather had the honor of serving as His late Majesty's envoy to your court. I accompanied him once to a meeting."

"Good Lord," Gerrold said, a little too loudly. "Is she their queen?"

"Ssh!" Annabel hissed. Lord Quinceton had managed, at least temporarily, to engage the nymphs and bring a halt to the dangerous turmoil in the river. He did not need distractions.

"Ah, that was your grandfather?" The nymph nodded slowly, then grinned. Her teeth were very white—and very pointed. "I do remember you. You were just an elver then."

He smiled back. "I compliment your memory, madam. I was indeed very small."

"And very delicious-looking. We wanted to keep you, as I recall." Her grin vanished abruptly. "Would you care to tell me why we should not keep these?" She lifted a webbed hand and gestured at the boys in the river. "Why have we not received our customary gifts? Is your grandfather ill?"

"My revered grandfather is many years gone, alas. I don't know why you haven't yet received a visit from the King's present representative, but I intend to find out. In the meanwhile, I hope you will condescend to accept a smaller gift as an earnest of our good will." He held out the tray.

The nymph frowned. "I don't see why we should, when we already have *them* to eat."

"You do, madam. But I venture to say that you might find these even more palatable—and that it is not behavior worthy of a queen to eat children in their mothers' sight." He indicated Annabel standing on the bank. She tried to look both deferential and anxious.

The nymph's eyes widened. "What? *All* these are her sons?"

Lord Quinceton opened his mouth, then closed it again and shot Annabel an amused look over his shoulder. "Indeed they are, madam."

"*What*?" Annabel almost dropped his clothes in the river. "They're not all mi—"

"Ssh," Watts hissed.

"Well." The nymph was clearly impressed. She

nodded to Annabel. "You are a good mother. I didn't know humans bore such litters."

She reached out and took a cake from the platter that Lord Quinceton offered her, sniffed at it suspiciously, then took a bite. "Oh," she said, and crammed the rest of it in her mouth. She gestured to her hitherto silent companion to take the platter, grabbing another cake as it passed her. "Do you have more of these?" she asked through a mouthful.

"More of those, and others as well," Lord Quinceton said. "If you will wait a moment, madam, I will have them brought out."

He turned and waded his way back to shore. "Get whoever is brave enough and start bringing those platters out," he said to Watts as he took the plate of sandwiches from Martin. "But send the rest to keep bringing in the boys."

"Yes, sir." Watts darted away.

"I can't *believe* you told her these were all my children!" Annabel said through gritted teeth.

He grinned. "I can't help it if she misunderstood me. Besides, your, er, fecundity impressed the old girl enough to make her stop and try the cakes, rather than nibbling a first former. Please, stand back," he called in a louder voice. The spectators on the bank had started to crowd toward them. "This isn't over yet. Please allow the boys with plates through."

In a very few minutes, Watts had gathered a handful of older boys to wade out with the plates of dainties brought by Martin's "men" and offer them to the nymphs who now drew close. They snatched happily at the macaroons, the glazed fruit, the chicken sandwiches, the cheese-cakes and lemon tarts, exclaiming to each other in their strange, gurgling language, while behind them other boys systematically ferried their stranded schoolmates into shore. When Martin's supplies ran out, other picnic baskets were ransacked by willing onlookers to keep the nymphs happily munching until all the boys had been brought in to safety. Lord Quinceton stood in waist-deep water, directing traffic to and from shore, until the nymph's leader swam toward him. He joined her in deeper water.

"Your gift was a good one," she said, licking icing off her webbed fingers. Annabel thought she might have polished off the entire plate of cakes by herself; wouldn't her cook, Mrs. Dailey, be flattered to hear that the queen of the Thames river nymphs admired her baking? Not that she was going to tell her about this afternoon's events—the poor woman would probably have a spasm.

"I am delighted that it found favor with you, madam," Lord Quinceton said, nodding his head.

"Not that we don't expect our regular tribute," the nymph queen added. "I think I want another plate of these when your man comes to parley with us."

"You shall have them."

"Good." She fixed him with her dark, pupil-less eyes. "But it is not good that this happened. We will permit it to pass because of you. But I will expect to receive your man soon. And he will not be late next year, or things will not go well for humans on the Thames." There was a cold implacability in her voice that gave Annabel the chills.

"I understand, madam—and give you my word that I will discover why this has happened and remedy it."

The nymph regarded him a moment longer, then nodded. "I will accept your word." She looked behind her, then made a gesture accompanied by a string of words. Several nymphs disappeared beneath the river's surface; a few moments later, the overturned boats that had drifted downstream could be seen making their way back up the river, along with bundles of oars. Watts' friends who'd helped bring the plates to the nymphs went out to receive the returned boats and bring them in to the bank.

"Thank you for that, madam," Lord Quinceton said. "The boats are precious to the boys."

"Are they?" She shrugged. "I just didn't want them clogging up my river." She gave a short cry, and the rest of the nymphs vanished under the water. "I will expect my tribute soon," she said to Lord Quinceton. Then she too was gone.

Martin had barely moved from Annabel's side, apart from relaying plates of food. Now he fetched a deep sigh. "Those ladies took everyone's serving platters and plates," he said.

Annabel laughed shakily and gave him a one-armed hug. "They're welcome to them, so long as your brother is safe." Where was Will? Surely all the boys had been accounted for, or—

"Well, Fellbridge?" Lord Quinceton had waded in from the river.

Annabel blinked at him standing before her, his dripping shirt plastered to him, the wet linen revealing his firmly muscled arms and torso with damp, loving exactitude. Oh, *my*. A rush of hot color flood her cheeks. "Er—Lord Quinceton—"

"Would you care to try squeezing the breath from me now? I do believe we had a wager to settle on that subject." He held his arms out to her, his eyes belying the innocent tone in his voice.

"I beg your pardon," she snapped. "It was not a wager!"

"Wasn't it? My mistake," he said meekly.

"Mama!"

The well-loved voice made her forget everything but the fact that her son was safe. She looked wildly about her. "Will! I'm here!"

A moment later, Will had wormed his way through the chattering spectators around her and hurtled toward her, nearly knocking her over.

"Oh, darling!" She bent to embrace him, not caring that he was both sodden and trailing streamers of river-weed caught in his buttons.

"William, if you do not keep this about you, I am convinced you will catch your death in those wet clothes." Mama hurried up behind him and draped a lap rug from Annabel's carriage over his shoulders.

"*An ounce of prevention is worth a pound of cure*, my boy." Papa brought up the rear. "I say," he said cheerfully to Lord Quinceton. "I'd heard of the Thames nymphs, of course, but never more than half-believed they were real. Just thought the King's Maintenancer was another royal sinecure to be handed out."

Mama ignored him. "You too," she said,

thrusting another lap rug at Lord Quinceton. "It would be a shame if the only man with the bottom to do anything about this disgraceful situation should succumb to an inflammation of the lungs."

"Yes, ma'am. Thank you, ma'am." Lord Quinceton meekly took the rug from her. Annabel felt an odd mixture of relief and regret as he draped it about his shoulders. "If Fellbridge can be convinced to part with my clothing, I promise I shall make myself respectable again as soon as I'm a little drier."

Annabel suddenly remembered that his coat, cravat, and waistcoat were still draped over her arm. She started to form a sharp retort, then met his eyes—and saw, above the teasing smile, that they held an expression of understanding. . . although understanding of what, she couldn't say. She mutely handed him his clothes, and to cover her confusion, embraced Will again.

"That was some quick thinking on your part, sir." Papa was still talking to Lord Quinceton. "Who knew they'd fancy a cake or two? Good thing you came prepared."

Mama coughed gently. Annabel opened her mouth to reply, but Martin spoke up. "He didn't bring all that food, sir. We did. Well," he added, after a moment's thought. "Us and the Sheltons and the Bowleses and the Beckets and—and a lot of others."

"The Beckets?" Papa's face turned red. "Are you saying that you just fed those nymphs their picnics?"

Martin nodded. "And yours, too," he added.

He began to splutter. "Why, you larcenous young imp—"

"Don't be silly, George. It was either that or allow those creatures to eat your grandson," Mama said briskly. "Did you really want that?"

Annabel shuddered and hugged both Will and Martin.

"I saved back a little bit of our picnic," Martin said in a small voice.

"And besides, there's still the champagne," Mama added.

Papa brightened. "Is there? Then I suppose we won't starve." He took Mama's arm and began to lead her back toward the field.

"Man does not live by wine alone," Lord Quinceton murmured in such a sanctimonious tone that Annabel was startled into a giggle.

Martin looked confused. "I thought it was, 'Man does not live by *bread* alone?'"

"It is," Will said. "Come on." He tugged his brother's arm, and they set out after their grandparents. "Did you save back any of Mrs. Dailey's cakes for us? I'm starving."

"He'll be over this in a trice, you know," Lord Quinceton commented as the boys broke into a run. "Do you wish to follow? I would offer you my arm but fear it is still wet."

Annabel looked at his proffered arm, which was indeed wet... and took it anyway. "I must thank you for having the wits to save my son, sir," she said, a little stiffly to cover her emotion. "Not to mention the rest of the boys."

"They weren't *my* wits. You were the one who

made the suggestion to invite the nymphs to picnic with us; I merely recognized its utility."

"Then I thank you for that."

"No need for further thanks, Fellbridge." There was a smile in his voice. "You've already done so, and handsomely."

"I have?" Annabel frowned. "How? I don't—"

"Quinceton!"

A small man, dressed more in country squire than town fashion, was striding toward them, hat in hand. As they approached, he paused and bowed. "Sir Edward Simms, at your service, sir. We have met once or twice at White's."

Lord Quinceton made a politely non-committal reply, but the man was too intent on his mission to notice. "I had to thank you for what you did this afternoon, sir, facing down those hags. My son was in one of the boats and doesn't swim a lick. You were as cool as a cucumber out there, by God! Didn't so much as blink an eyelash!" He took Lord Quinceton's hand and wrung it. "My boy's alive and well, thanks to you. Wait till they hear about this at White's! You'll be stood your weight in toasts, I'll warrant—"

"No, I will most emphatically not," Lord Quinceton said, quietly but very clearly.

"What?" Sir Edward dropped his hand and began to bristle.

"If you feel the need to thank me, you may do so by *not* talking about what happened today, at White's or anywhere."

The man looked astonished. "But—why?"

"What happened here has. . . ramifications

that are not readily apparent. Ramifications of concern to His Majesty's government. Today's events will be a matter of discussion at very high levels indeed; gossip about it will not be welcomed, nor will it help anyone involved." He fixed Sir Edward with a stern look. "So while I accept your thanks, I hope that any further discussion of the event on your part—and everyone else who witnessed it—comes to an end here and now."

Sir Edward gulped and nodded. "I—I understand, my lord. Not another word." He bowed again, awkwardly, and hurried away.

Lord Quinceton sighed. "I was afraid that would happen."

"You can scarcely blame him, can you? How often does one see a river full of rampaging river nymphs threatening to eat the students of Eton?"

He smiled reluctantly. "Not very often, I'll grant you that. But this should not become the chief topic of conversation in London's clubs and ballrooms this coming week. It is far too delicate a matter."

She nodded. However, it would certainly be a topic of conversation in one London venue tomorrow: she and Maria would be informing the Lady Patronesses of the day's events.

He sighed again. "I can see I shall have to spend the rest of the afternoon talking to all the Sir Edwards here."

"I expect my father would help you. He loves to have an excuse to talk to people."

"Spoken like a dutiful daughter." He smiled at her sideways. "I am glad to see that you can speak lightly about the Potamides."

"I couldn't have a half-hour ago." Annabel couldn't repress a shudder.

"But you can now. You're a woman of eminently good sense as well as good looks. . . but I already knew that."

Annabel blushed.

---

"I have been thinking, daughter," Papa began, pouring himself another glass of champagne.

"Oh dear," Mama said under her breath.

"What have you been thinking, sir?" Annabel held out her glass for him to refill. She suspected she would need it.

They had found the table and chairs her footman John had put out for them, with cushions and her third-best linens and china, and nibbled through the food Martin had left, washing it down with liberal amounts of champagne. Annabel was grateful for that; whilst she could joke about the river nymphs, the thought of them still left a chill inside her that the champagne had gone only a little way toward banishing. Watts and Gerrold had joined them for a while, behaving like boys invited to their first grown-up party.

Lord Quinceton had indeed cajoled Papa into wandering about the picnicking groups, cautioning them not to discuss the river nymphs back in town. Lord Sefton had helped, and the other members of the House of Lords present had added their voices to theirs. With any luck, the story would not become the latest *on-dit*.

And now the three boys—for Gus had joined them—were running about the field shouting and carrying on with their friends. The sight of that did even more than the champagne to warm her.

Papa was evidently watching them too. "Those grandsons of mine. Look at them, running around as if they were heathen savages!" He gestured with his glass, slopping a little champagne onto the grass. "Back when I was a boy, we never did such a thing."

"Indeed not!" Mama said. "I believe you and your brothers ran about like *Christian* savages."

He looked down his nose at her. "As you were not there, madam, I do not understand how you can say such a thing."

"Your mother told me." She gave him her sweetest smile. "And Grandmother Shellingham would *never* lie. Besides, all work and no play makes Jack a dull boy."

Papa harrumphed. "Be that as it may. . . Annabel, those boys need a firm masculine hand to rein them in. Appropriating everyone's picnics without so much as a by-your-leave and selling them off! I don't care if it was for a good cause," he said as she opened her mouth to protest. "They should not have done it. It's high time you married again and gave those boys a father."

"Papa!" She had been *very* right to fortify herself with more champagne.

"Oh, George." Mama closed her eyes and winced as if she had the headache.

"I quite agree with you, sir," Lord Quinceton said.

*"What!?"* Annabel almost dropped her glass.

He gave her the blandest of looks. "I was merely agreeing that your sons would indeed benefit from frequent exposure to the good example of a wise, responsible older male."

Mama made a small, peculiar choking sound.

"Precisely!" Papa beamed at him.

"Oh?" Annabel narrowed her eyes at him. "And just which 'wise, responsible older male' would you suggest should be frequently exposed to my sons?"

"Why, their grandfather, of course. Who better to set a good example for the coming generation? Upon consideration, sir, you perhaps ought to consider setting aside the champagne. I'm not persuaded it sets the example for your grandsons that you might wish."

Papa, who'd been draining his glass, coughed and sputtered. Mama pounded him on the back, not bothering to conceal her smile. "Pray inform me, sir," she said to Lord Quinceton, "whether you take more pleasure from quizzing my husband or my daughter."

He returned her smile. "At any other time, I would be pleased to oblige you, ma'am, but fear the answer would just get me into more trouble."

"Very likely," Annabel said darkly, but something in the twinkle in Lord Quinceton's eyes would not allow her to maintain her frown. She looked away, an unwilling smile tugging at the corners of her mouth.

Papa finally caught his breath and looked up at the darkening sky. "It's probably time we got back to the Brocas. They'll be starting the fireworks soon." The boys who had rowed, including Will, were already gathering at the river's edge near their boats, joking and jostling as if the day's earlier events had not happened.

"I am *not* walking this time," Mama said firmly.

"Of course not. We shall drive, of course." Annabel rose and gestured to John to begin to pack away their picnic, then waved to Martin. "It's time to go, if you would care for a ride to the Brocas," she called.

"Except there won't be any room for you, dear, if Martin and his friend come with us in the landau," Mama said as they began to stroll in the direction of the carriages. "So you shall have to go with Lord Quinceton."

"Just what I was thinking, ma'am," he agreed.

When had the pair of them become so thick? Annabel was about to ask why *she* didn't accompany him when Mama spoke again.

"Annabel, my love, your dress is quite ruined, you know," she said, surveying Annabel critically.

Annabel looked down at herself. If not sodden, her front was still damp and wrinkled from hugging the very wet Will—was that a stray bit of river-weed?—and her hem was definitely soaked from passing trays of cakes to Lord Quinceton and the others. She did not even want to know how much dust and dirt decorated the back of her skirt, courtesy of the fiery-footed Diablo. "Yes, it is," she said with a sigh. "Winters will be very cross with me."

"Can you blame her? That dress is beyond redemption, and I'll wager the poor thing probably never gets any of your cast-offs to sell because you two are so diligent about making your dresses over."

Annabel cringed. Did Mama have to say such things in front of Lord Quinceton? He knew she had to scrimp—everyone knew it—but to make an announcement of it was the outside of enough.

"Well, never mind," Mama continued. "I shall take you shopping for a new one tomorrow; your father will be occupied with showing off his new carriage."

"You don't have to do that—"

"Nonsense. I shall be at loose ends whilst he peacocks about Hyde Park with his friends." She ignored Papa's indignant protest. "Oh, but you have your Almack's meeting in the morning, don't you? Afterward, then. My mantua-maker will be delighted to see us."

"I have often thought, ma'am, that pink is a most advantageous color for your daughter," Lord Quinceton offered.

Mama stopped walking and examined Annabel consideringly. "Yes, I do believe you are correct."

He paused as well. "Nothing too pale."

"Oh, no. Pale pink is far too insipid. Something darker, perhaps with an apricot tinge."

"Exactly as you say, Lady Shellingham."

"Or cinnamon. A cinnamon pink might look well."

"I think either would do admirably."

Annabel looked at the pair of them standing side by side and staring at her, nodding slowly and in such mutual understanding that she could not decide whether to laugh or shriek. "Are you two quite finished?"

"Annabel!" Mama pretended to look hurt. "We're only trying to *help*."

"Finished? Never, Fellbridge." Lord Quinceton offered her his arm to lead her to his curricle.

## Chapter Five

The Tuesday afternoon after the Fourth of June was cloudy, but no rain threatened Annabel and her mother as they strolled in Hyde Park, talking desultorily and smiling and waving whenever Papa went by in his new barouche. He'd had a different companion for each circuit; Mama applauded his efficiency in managing to show off to the maximum number of friends and acquaintances in the smallest amount of time.

"I knew he would begin to get impatient to return to his roses, no matter how excited he was about his carriage," she commented. "That's why I was anxious to get our shopping completed."

"Completed? We don't have five more milliners and three more glove shops to visit?"

"Don't be cheeky, dear," Mama said imperturbably. "I probably shan't have the opportunity to return to town until October, so I had to stock up. And there was that small matter of your dress."

Or rather, dress*es*. Upon her return from her Almack's meeting yesterday, Annabel had found Mama closeted with Winters, the two of them resembling a pair of generals planning a protracted military campaign. Before she could do more than quickly use the water closet, Mama had whisked her off, clutching a list she and Winters had evidently made and which she wouldn't allow Annabel to see.

By late afternoon Annabel had been fitted for a new walking dress to replace the one she'd ruined the day before—as well as a carriage dress and two evening dresses. Three of the four were in shades of pink, as was the lace- and ribbon-trimmed satin dressing gown which Mama insisted upon buying her.

"Mama, I don't *need* all these," she whispered as Mama's mantua-maker, Mrs. Carpenter, happily wrote up the order.

"Yes, you do. Poor Winters will be chuffed to have something new to dress you in—you don't want to deny her that pleasure, do you?" Mama opened her eyes very wide.

Annabel sighed. "Mama, you're being manipulative. It's not fair."

"It's for a good cause, dear. Trust me."

If she were to be honest, Annabel could not help being a little pleased at Mama's gift—well, perhaps more than a little if honesty truly were to be respected. Who would not be at the thought of four lovely new dresses, plus two hats, two pairs of slippers dyed to match the evening gowns, and six new pairs of silk stockings? Precisely *why* Mama had insisted on all the pink was not a question she wanted to delve into too closely.

Mama consulted the watch pinned to her bodice, then glanced behind them. "Hmm," she said.

"What is it? Did you have an appointment somewhere?"

"No, of course not. I was just thinking what a useful name Carpenter is for a mantua-maker. Only think—when French things are in fashion, she can become Madame Charpentier with very little trouble. Since the war is going so badly, I suppose that's why she's plain Mrs. Carpenter for now. Still, I think it's very clever of her."

"Marrying a man named Carpenter had nothing to do with it, I suppose." Mama could say the most marvelously ridiculous things sometimes. "However, I rather doubt there is a Mr. Carpenter unless his present abode is the churchyard. She's far too good a businesswoman to allow a husband to hover in the background. I will allow that perhaps her father was named Carpenter."

Mama's brows delicately knit themselves. "I hadn't considered that."

Annabel was about to reply, but a carriage slowing to match their pace distracted her. She looked up to see Lord Quinceton sweeping his hat off in salute. Unusually, a groom rode beside him.

"Good afternoon, Lady Shellingham. I passed your husband a few minutes ago, wearing an expression of the most becoming modesty as he drove his new barouche with Lord Wrayne beside him." He nodded to Annabel, eyebrows raised inquiringly. "Fellbridge, I see you are quite recovered, at least outwardly."

Mama stopped walking, forcing him to halt as well. "Why, Lord Quinceton, what a *surprise* to see you here!"

The unfurling of a small, suspicious thought made Annabel say, "Is it?"

Mama ignored her. "I am very glad to see you, sir. I was just noticing that I'm really quite fatigued and would prefer to return to our hotel, but I don't want to cut short Annabel's enjoyment of the day. I would be much obliged if you would take her up and permit your groom to wait with me until Lord Shellingham chances by again."

The suspicion transformed into a certainty. Good Lord, Mama had *planned* this. But how? She would have had to send Lord Quinceton a note arranging the meeting, and—

"Nothing would afford me greater pleasure, ma'am." He nodded to his groom.

"Mama, you are quite beyond anything," Annabel said. The groom leapt down and went to the horses' heads; Lord Quinceton leaned over and held out his hand to help her into the vacated seat. "And so are you, sir!" she added severely when she was seated beside him.

He tucked the lap robe over her. "I'll take that as a compliment."

"We'll see you at Grillon's at seven for dinner, dear," Mama said as he gathered up the reins again. "Have a lovely drive!"

Lord Quinceton was silent for a few moments

as they eased into the flow of promenading carriages. "Your mother is a remarkable woman," he finally said.

"My mother should be *hanged*." Annabel was still seething.

He laughed. "Oh, come now, Fellbridge. Is it really all that bad? Just say the word, and I shall set you down at once." When she did not reply he added, "If it makes you feel any better, I dared not disregard her directions about meeting you this afternoon. She threatened to be *disappointed* in me."

That drew an unwilling smile from her. "It's just. . . embarrassing."

"It shouldn't be. She's so charming about it that I certainly don't mind. She has much more finesse than my mother when she tries her hand at the same game."

How did she not know his mother? "I don't believe I've ever met Lady Quinceton."

"That's because she's no longer Lady Quinceton. She married Lord Ballymena a few years after my father's death and moved to Ireland. She comes to England only rarely."

Was it only Annabel's imagination that she thought she heard him add, "Thank God!" under his breath? Before she could decide he said, "I fell in with your mother's plans so readily because I had hoped to have an opportunity to speak with you."

"On what topic?"

"The expected one, I suppose—what happened at Eton." He slowed his team a little and looked at her earnestly. "More specifically, the Potamides and the King's Maintenancer."

"What about them?"

"Just this: are you planning to 'investigate' them?"

"Goodness, no! Why should I want to do that?"

He frowned. "That won't fadge, ma'am. I know you too well. After what your son went through, I would expect you'd be preparing to—pardon my language—investigate the devil out of them."

"Well, I'm not." Oh, they certainly would be investigated—but not by her.

At yesterday's Lady Patronesses' meeting, Maria had acquainted everyone with the previous day's events at Eton, with Annabel supplying details. There had been smiles at Lord Quinceton's unusual but effective method of dealing with the immediate crisis as well as several expressions of surprise: Annabel was glad to see she wasn't the only one who hadn't known about the Potamides' existence.

No one had been amused, however, by the news that the king's appointed representative, Lord Rossing, was not performing his Maintenancing duties.

"Needless to say, this could become a serious problem," Maria said. "Not just on the Thames but on other rivers as well."

"I don't quite know what to say, since I hadn't even heard of the Potamides before this," Sally said. She sounded peeved about the fact. "Which I suppose should not be too surprising since it's a

Crown matter. But that very thing puts it beyond our purview, does it not? And if Lord Quinceton is aware of the problem, won't he be able to report it?"

"I should care to know to *whom* he will report it," Dorothea said. "Certainly not to this Lord Rossing, whom I do not know and do not wish to know."

"Maria and Georgiana knew about the Potamides already. What do they think?" Clementina asked.

Georgiana and Maria exchanged glances. Then Georgiana said, "I agree that this is not our business and we should not try to involve ourselves—in any *official* way."

Sally nodded. "But unofficially, perhaps? Information is always useful to us."

"Information about Lord Rossing?" Frances was in attendance that morning. Annabel had not yet had the opportunity to ask how her aunt did; at any event, the lack of mourning implied that the lady lingered yet. "Oh, I think he might be an acquaintance of my brother's, but I am not sure. I had no idea about these Poma—no, Po*ta*mides. Shall I see what I can discover about him?"

Sally looked relieved. "Yes, please, Frances. And thank you for telling us about this, ladies. Annabel, I'm very glad that your son was not hurt."

"So am I," Annabel agreed fervently.

After the meeting Frances had gone straight to her. "Annabel! What a dreadful thing that must have been at Eton yesterday! Your poor son! Oh, I do wish I had been there to see Quin vanquish those horrid creatures!"

"He didn't vanquish them—he fed them." Did Frances have to be so *obvious* about her infatuation with him? "How is your great-aunt, by the way? Is she on the mend?"

"My—oh, yes, my aunt." Frances shook her head. "No change, really. Thankfully, her physician doesn't think we should give up hope of a recovery just yet. But you must tell me all about yesterday— what did Quin do? What did he say? He's so clever! And *brave*!"

The brave and clever Lord Quinceton sighed, recalling Annabel to the moment. "I promise I haven't the least interest in investigating Lord Rossing or anything to do with him," she said firmly.

"I am relieved to hear you say that. This is not a matter that you should be concerning yourself with. In *any* way."

"Yes, I—I had come to that conclusion."

He looked at her. "Why does that answer fail to fill me with confidence?"

"Don't be horrid. I don't want to even hear the words 'river nymph' again for as long as I live. And anyway, I fully intend to have some fun in the next few days. I am going to Epsom for the races tomorrow."

"Oh?" He sounded surprised. "I did not know you were a racing enthusiast."

"I'm not. But several friends are going—it seems there's a wonder horse everyone's talking about who's supposed to be running, and I thought, 'why not?'"

That wasn't quite true. She was indeed going

to Epsom, but not purely for fun. Mr. Almack had reported a possible matter of investigation at the annual race meet, and Georgiana and Maria had been assigned to investigate, with Annabel to assist as needed.

"Then perhaps I will see you there. I usually stop in for a day or so." He hesitated. "May I ask you a question without fear of giving offence?"

"You may certainly *ask*, sir."

"Whether I get an answer is another issue?" He smiled. "Fair enough. I hope you aren't thinking of trying to, er, raise some capital at Epsom?"

"What, bet on races?" Annabel laughed. "No, not at all. I wouldn't have the first idea of how to choose a horse to bet on."

"Your husband didn't either, but he never allowed that to stop him."

Freddy *had* always gone to Epsom, hadn't he? She'd assumed it was because it was what gentlemen did—and this race meet was very fashionable. That he was gambling heavily as well as carousing with his friends hadn't really occurred to her. "No," she said quietly. "I won't be placing bets."

They drove in silence for a moment. Then she said, "May I ask *you* a question without fear of giving offense?"

"Ask away, Fellbridge. I am notoriously difficult to offend."

"I am glad to hear that. At Eton—no, it's nothing to do with the Potamides or the King's Maintenancer," she said quickly as his brows drew together.

"What, then?"

She took a breath. "What was your meaning yesterday when you said that Gus Blackburn had been taken care of?"

"Oh, that." He laughed softly.

"Yes, that." His laugh nettled her. "The boy is in a sad position and may not be able to continue at Eton—"

"He'll be able to stay at Eton as long as he likes. I had a talk with the new Head—Keate, is it?—in May, and we were able to come to an agreement."

An *agreement*? "Are you saying that *you're* paying his tuition?"

"Er, yes, I am. Room and board and his other classes as well, as I recall. I left it up to Keate to arrange the details and send them to my steward."

It took her a moment to recover from her astonishment. "But—that is, you don't know him, do you? No, of course not. You didn't even recognize him on Sunday when he came to speak with me."

"No, I hadn't yet laid eyes on the boy," he agreed.

There was an amused note in his voice that Annabel knew—and mistrusted. But she couldn't withdraw now. "Then why are you paying for his schooling?"

He shrugged. "Because it seemed to matter to you."

She just managed not to gasp. He was paying Gus's fees—for her sake? A gulf of meaning suddenly yawned at her feet; did she dare look into it?

"Yes, it does matter to me. Thank you," she

finally said. Her voice sounded stiff even in her own ears. "When I am in better frame, I trust you will allow me to reimburse you for your trouble."

"You? Never. If Master Blackburn wishes to do so at some later date, I will accept it if he wishes, but don't intend to ask for it. In the meanwhile, I am arranging a method of compensation with him that I expect will be satisfactory to both of us."

"But—"

"But if you should care to thank me, Fellbridge, there's one way you can."

"How?"

He smiled again, but there was no mockery or teasing in it this time. "At one point on Sunday, you addressed me in less formal terms than you usually do."

"I. . . don't know what you're talking about."

"Just before I went into the river, you called me Quin. Not 'Lord Quinceton' as is your wont."

She swallowed. "Did I?"

"Yes, you did. I confess to having felt some elation, as it implied that you were perhaps thinking of me in friendlier terms than you did a month or two ago."

Her face grew hot. Any moment now, the feather from her hat sweeping against her cheek would burst into flame. "I—uh. . . that is—"

He ignored her. "At the time, I took it as thanks for getting your son out of trouble. But I would not be averse to hearing you use it more often." He paused, then added, very gently, "Please?"

I hope you enjoyed the fifth installment of *The Ladies of Almack's*! There's more—much more!—to come. Keep reading for a sample of the next story, *An Event at Epsom*. And if you'd like to keep up with the news from King Street, sign up for my newsletter for new release announcements, extras, and more about the ladies:

https://marissadoylenewsletter.link/

Also, if you enjoyed reading *Turmoil on the Thames*, please consider telling your friends who might also enjoy it or posting a review on the site where you purchased it or on your favorite social media site such as Goodreads or LibraryThing.

# Author's Note

Please note that any resemblance between a certain event in Chapter 4 to a well-known aquatic moment in a popular and well-loved Jane Austen television mini-series is of course *purely* coincidental.

## A little background on Eton College

Eton College was founded by King Henry VI in 1440 as a charity school for deserving poor boys, to prepare them to enter King's College at Cambridge. While its continued existence seemed in doubt in the years after its founding, it eventually became one of the best known and most prestigious of boys' boarding schools. Of course, any institution that has been around for centuries acquires its own culture and history. We know about the Fourth of June (still part of the social calendar, by the way), but here's the skinny on a few other bits of Eton history and custom mentioned in this story:

- *Eton slang - dry bobs:* When a place has been around as long as Eton has, it not surprisingly collects a vast amount of folklore, traditions, and slang. One of those slang terms is "dry bobs", which Quin uses when addressing Martin and his co-conspirators. It means boys who prefer cricket (played on dry land, obviously) to rowing. If Martin was a dry bob, his twin Will, out on the river, was a "wet bob."

- *Montem*: Eton Montem (or Ad Montem) was another tradition observed from the 16th century to the 19th (it was abolished in 1847.) Originally it seems to have been a sort of initiation rite for new boys, conducted at the Montem Mound, or Salt Hill, a couple of miles from the college. It eventually evolved (or devolved) into a good-natured sort of highway robbery, when carriages and horsemen on the nearby Bath road would be stopped on Montem day (sometime in May or June, depending on the ecclesiastical calendar) by groups of boys demanding a payment in order to be allowed to go on; the money thus raised was for the Senior Colleger's anticipated expenses at university. By the 1770s it was only held once every three years but was attended by luminaries including George IV and, later, Queen Victoria and Prince Albert. The birth and growth of the railway system spelled its death sentence: so many rowdy crowds came out from London for it in 1841 and 1844 that Eton's headmaster abolished it before the 1847 celebration.

- *Lodgings for boys Oppidans/Collegers:* Until recent times (again relatively speaking, considering how old Eton is), a large proportion of boys attending Eton lived in boarding houses in town outside of the school, often run by respectable widows or by Eton teachers as a side gig, which provided room and board—hence Annabel's concern that their house "dame" (in quotes, because dames could be male or female) was not feeding her sons sufficiently. Boys who lived in these boarding houses were known as *Oppidans*, from the Latin word for "town." *Collegers* were boys who lived on campus; they were scholarship students as per the original foundation of the school who were guaranteed admission to King's College, Cambridge, on completing their education at Eton. By later in the 19th century, this system had broken down in favor of school-run "houses" for all students.

## Making one's curtsey to the queen

When a young lady of means was considered to be of marriageable age—the number varied but was generally at least seventeen—she "came out" to society in order to meet possible appropriate husbands. This meant parties and dinners and balls and (if she were lucky and well-born) vouchers to Almack's. And (again) if she was well-born and well-connected, she might be presented to the queen at court. Being presented was not strictly a requirement for being "out", but one could not be invited to parties given by the king and queen (or, shortly, the Prince Regent) if one had not been presented. So you can imagine that young persons entering society (yes, young men were presented as well) did not want to run the risk of being excluded if they had any social pretensions at all.

## The Duke of Cumberland incident

George III's fifth son, Ernest, Duke of Cumberland, was one of the least popular of the king's unpopular sons. Unlike most of his brothers who were on the plump side, Ernest took after his mother and was rail-thin; a saber cut down one side of his face, received when he fought the French in Holland at the Battle of Tournai, gave him a rather sinister appearance despite his handsome features. And unlike all his brothers, he was an avowed Tory and never dabbled in Whiggery or any liberal causes, being particularly opposed to Catholic Emancipation. He had an unpleasant reputation from his Army days as being a savage disciplinarian, and rumors about his personal life were rife.

But those rumors were nothing compared to the gossip that ricocheted around London after the wee hours of May 31, 1810.

According to the duke, he went to bed around

one a.m. in his apartments at St. James Palace after attending a concert earlier in the evening. He stated that he was awakened by two blows to his head, then quickly received four other blows and a saber cut to his thigh as he tried to flee to the room of one of his valets, Neale, calling out that he had been murdered. Though a small lamp burned in his room, he said he saw no one. The valet dashed to his master's defense, waving a poker about, until he tripped over a sword—the duke's own, covered with a considerable amount of blood. While Neale tended to his master, the duke requested that his other valet, Joseph Sellis, a native of Corsica, be summoned as well. When the servants went to Sellis's room, they found the door was locked. After various backing and forthing involving doors that should have been locked but weren't, Sellis's room was finally gained—and Sellis himself found with his throat slit by a razor. There was no sign of a struggle.

*Ew.*

So what had actually happened?

The jury called to hear the incident's inquest found, on weighing the extensive testimony and physical evidence, that Sellis had attacked his master and then committed suicide. Based on the accounts given by all the servants, that was probably what happened, though we'll never know what inspired the attack.

But public opinion whispered otherwise— remember how disliked the duke was? It was rumored that the duke had seduced Sellis's wife, and murdered Sellis when the valet threatened to go public with his knowledge, then arranged matters to look as though he had been attacked instead. Other rumors postulated an affair between the duke and Sellis, and that the duke had murdered him when he threatened blackmail, while others favored the theory that Sellis had discovered an affair between the duke and his other valet, and was murdered by the duke in order to keep the affair secret. Some who accepted that Sellis had indeed attempted to murder his master suggested that he had done so in revenge for the duke's seduction of his wife. Others guessed that he was tired of the duke's constant stream of anti-Catholic jokes and mockery (Sellis was Catholic) and had simply had *enough*.

The duke survived, though it took months for him to recover (his brain could actually be seen through one of the wounds in his head, and his thumb had nearly been severed by the saber.) His reputation, however, never recovered, and he would go on to be accused of even worse things, such as being the father of his own sister's illegitimate child and of scheming to bring about the death of his niece Victoria, who until she had children was all that stood between the duke and the crown.

Makes the royal scandals of today look pretty tame, doesn't it?

## The Duke of York and his mistress

The king's second son, Frederick, Duke of York, was also (like his younger brother the Duke of Cumberland), a soldier. . . in fact, he was named commander-in-chief of the British Army in 1798.

Though he wasn't perhaps the most inspired field commander, he was a more-than-able administrator, and his reforms of the army's structure and management were likely just as responsible as the Duke of Wellington's strategic genius for Britain's ultimate victory over Napoleon.

But in 1809-1810, that was all in the future... and no one would have believed the duke was any good as an administrator either, for he was neck-deep in scandal.

Like most of his brothers, the duke was a ladies' man. Though fond of his wife, Frederica of Prussia, he generally had a mistress in his keeping, and in 1803 that mistress was Mary Anne Clarke, a popular courtesan (and an ancestress of Daphne du Maurier.) Mary Anne's tastes were expensive; though the duke had set her up in her own house with an allowance of £100 per month, she was spending at five times that rate. To supplement her income, she hit on the scheme of using her position as the duke's *belle amie* to sell army commissions, promotions, and transfers to the highest bidders, undercutting the government, which was also in the same business (yes, at the time, that was how things worked): she'd take the money and see that the names were added to the lists to be approved by the duke. Word eventually got out, and a formal committee was set up by Parliament to look into the matter. The duke sent Mary Anne packing and resigned his position as commander-in-chief; he was reinstated a while later after the commission found that while he was aware of Mary Anne's activities, he himself had not benefited financially from them. Mary Anne managed to negotiate a good pension from the royal family after threatening to publish the duke's love letters to her, and after the war eventually moved to France, where she lived comfortably until her death in 1852.

## Ladies' maids and cast-off dresses

While most servants did not make very much in salary, many positions had traditional perquisites attached to them that could prove quite lucrative. Butlers, for example, could claim candle ends and empty bottles to sell; cooks could sell dripping saved from the cooking of meat; while this sounds strange to modern ears, a comfortable sum could be accumulated from these activities.

Personal servants—ladies' maids and valets—probably had the best perks: it was generally accepted that they could lay claim to their employers' cast-off clothes, either to sell to second-hand clothing dealers, to send home to family and friends, or to modify for themselves. Annabel's maid, Winters, likely doesn't get much of her mistress's cast-offs, as Lady Shellingham observes.

## The King's Maintenancer of the Tamesian Potamides

This office of course does not exist (at least, I don't think it does.) But there are any number of royal offices with similar obscure names and purposes left over from the Middle Ages, my favorite being the Queen's (or King's) Swan Marker and Swan

Uppers, whose job it is to perform an annual count of the swans on the Thames, which (nominally) belong to the Crown.

# Dramatis Personae

## Or, a brief list of who was *really* who

For those among you who are not hard-core Regency fanatics, the following are highly idiosyncratic biographical sketches of the historical figures mentioned in this first story.

## But first, a quickie tutorial on title usage in England

Peers (anyone of the rank of baron, viscount, earl, marquis, or duke) have a family name or surname like their less exalted fellow humans, but then also have their title, and can be referred to by both. Let's look at an example...

John Smith is the Earl of Noodle. He is commonly known as Lord Noodle; his friends might just call him Noodle, or he might be referred to as John

Noodle to differentiate him from his late father, George Noodle, if the family is being gossip-ed about. . . but Noodle is not his surname—that's Smith. He will never be referred to as Lord John Smith or Lord John Noodle; men referred to as "Lord First-name Surname" are usually the younger sons of marquises and dukes, who are given the courtesy title of "Lord."

His wife, Mary Smith, the Countess of Noodle, is commonly known as Lady Noodle; she might be referred to as Mary Noodle to differentiate her from her mother-in-law Jane, the Dowager Countess, who is still alive and gadding about in society, and the name might stick even after the Dowager countess is no more just because everyone has gotten used to it. Mary will *not* be called Lady Mary Noodle, or Lady Mary Smith; women referred to as "Lady First-name Surname" are the daughters of the higher nobility—earls and above—and are permitted the use of the courtesy title of "Lady." A widow of a peer keeps her rank and title unless she remarries, when she then takes her new husband's rank (and title, if any.) In social practice, many women who married men of lower rank still kept the courtesy title they were born with.

Fred Smith, Viscount Macaroni, is Lord Noodle's eldest son. Most members of the higher nobility have multiple titles, so an eldest son (and ONLY an eldest son—there are a whole set of rules around heirs apparent—direct offspring—and heirs presumptive—brothers and nephews and cousins—that we won't get into right now) is permitted to "borrow" his father's second most prestigious title as a courtesy (though if there is a third title and if Fred has a son, the lad might get to use that one if grandpa allowed it.) Fred's younger brothers are just plain Honourables (only younger sons of marquises and dukes use the courtesy title of "Lord", don't forget) but his sister is Lady Susan because the daughters of earls (and marquises and dukes) have the courtesy title of "Lady."

There are other rules—dukes have their own special set. So...

Aurelius Smith is the Duke of Megapounds. Unlike his cousin John Smith, Earl of Noodle, he is *never* known as *Lord* Megapounds. He might be addressed just by his title, Megapounds, by his friends and acquaintances... or he might be addressed as "Duke" by others of his (relative) social class or as "your grace" by his inferiors. When he's being gossiped about, he might be referred to as Aurelius Megapounds or as "the seventh Duke" to differentiate him from his father Julius Megapounds, the sixth Duke. Aurelius's wife Ruby Smith, the Duchess of Megapounds, is likewise addressed as "Duchess" by friends and acquaintances, or as "your grace" by her inferiors, or as Ruby Megapounds to differentiate her from her mother-in-law the dowager duchess, Pearl Megapounds.

Now for the who's who...

Sally Jersey

Sarah Sophia Child Villiers, Countess of Jersey

(1785-1867), known as Sally Jersey to differentiate her from her mother-in-law, also Lady Jersey (and well-known as a mistress of the Prince of Wales). She was also known by the ironic nickname "Silence" as she was reputed never to stop talking, and was a Lady Patroness of Almack's and very influential in society for many years, though never as actively interested in politics as were many of the other Lady Patronesses. Fascinatingly, she inherited the senior partnership in a bank—Child & Co.—from her maternal grandfather (as well as his fortune—she was one wealthy woman!) and on attaining the age of 21 took her role very seriously and was active in the bank's management for her entire life. She is reputed to have had many love affairs, including one with Henry "Cupid" Templeton, Emily Cowper's squeeze.

## Georgiana Bathurst

Georgiana Bathurst, Countess Bathurst (one of the exceptions to all my rules above; in this case, the title and family surname were the same), 1765-1841. Georgiana was born a member of the Lennox family, descended from King Charles II and his mistress Louise de Kérouaille, and niece to the famous Lennox sisters, one of who nearly married George III. Aside from the basic information around her ancestry, her marriage to the 3rd Earl Bathurst who held several government positions, a list of her children, and the fact that she served as a Lady Patroness, almost no information about her seems to be available... which left me free to create a personality for her.

## Emily Cowper (pronounced "cooper," just so you know)

Emily Mary Cowper, Countess Cowper (another exception where the surname and title coincide), 1787-1869. Born Emily Lamb, daughter of the well-known Lady Melbourne (another mistress of the Prince of Wales), brother of William Lamb, later Viscount Melbourne, Queen Victoria's first prime minister, and sister-in-law of crazy-cakes Caro Lamb, lover of Lord Byron. She was married at a young age to Peter Clavering-Cowper, 5th Earl Cowper who was ten years her senior. She bore him a son, then embarked on a series of love affairs in London while he remained more or less contentedly in the country at their estate in Hertfordshire. Her grand passion was Henry John "Cupid" Temple, 3rd Viscount Palmerston, who was the probable father of a few of her children and whom she married in 1839 after her first husband's death. She was a political hostess *par excellence,* being the sister of one Prime Minister and the wife of another. She was one of the most popular of the Lady Patronesses, known for her kindness and social *élan.*

## Clementina Sarah Drummond-Burrell

Clementina Sarah Drummond-Burrell, later Lady Willoughby de Eresby, 1786-1865. Clementina was a Scottish heiress and daughter of an earl; her husband, Peter Burrell, added her last name to his own so that they became known as Mr. and Mrs. Drummond-Burrell. Later her husband inherited a pair of baronies from both his father and (unusually) his mother; the older, more prestigious title was his mother's Willoughby de Eresby one, so that's the one they used. While Peter pursued a political career which Clementina's fortune subsidized (as well as his habits as a dandy), Clementina pursued a social one, becoming a hostess of some renown. She was reputed to be proud and haughty in nature and a stickler for correct behavior, which inspired the power I gave her, though some historians contend that it was her mother-in-law, not her, who was so snooty. Unusually for the time (and among her fellow Lady Patronesses) Clementina's marital reputation remained unstained, and she and her husband appear to have enjoyed a faithful, devoted relationship.

## Maria Sefton

Maria Molyneux, Viscountess Sefton and later Countess of Sefton, 1769-1851. While much is known about her husband William's career as both a politician and a noted friend of the Prince of Wales (as well as a founder of the exclusive Four-in-Hand Club), very little is known about Maria beyond her connection with Almack's as a Lady Patroness. Might that excessive prudence be a function of the fact that her parents, Lord and Lady Craven, had both lived rather scandalous lives and had divorced, a rarity at the time? She was reputed to be extremely good-natured, however, and an excellent if self-effacing hostess for her busy husband.

## Dorothea Lieven

Dorothea von Lieven, Countess (and later Princess) Lieven, 1785-1857. Born in Riga, Latvia, Dorothea was a Russo-German noblewoman (she was educated at a convent in Russia and served as a maid-of-honor to the Tsar's mother) who was married (at age 14!) to General Count Christopher von Lieven. He was sent by Tsar Alexander I to serve as the Imperial Ambassador to England in 1812 (ssh, yes, I know that's two years after the setting of my stories. I invoke my creative license.) Dorothea took to London like a duck to water. She adored politics, knew everyone, and was the first foreigner asked to serve as a Lady Patroness at Almack's. She was known to be haughty and snobbish, had multiple affairs (including one with Count Metternich of Austria and again with "Cupid" Palmerston), received her own secret diplomatic assignments from the Tsar, and generally had a grand time of it for twenty years, until her husband was recalled to Russia. Not long after she left him to live in Paris, where she established a salon and went on her merry way with a finger in every diplomatic pie until her death.

## William Almack/Mr. Willis

Although he is referred to by contemporaries as a

Scot, it's not known either when or where William Almack was born (though Thirsk in Yorkshire is a likely bet—so, not Scottish but perhaps of Scottish ancestry.) The earliest reports of him are as valet to the Duke of Hamilton, but he soon went into business as a proprietor of a tavern and then as owner-manager of a gaming club in Pall Mall to which he gave his own name—and which eventually became known as Brooks's, one of the best known of London's men's clubs and still in operation today. In 1764 he built his famous Assembly Rooms in King Street and gathered his Lady Patronesses to administer them. . . though perhaps not in quite the way told in this story! On his death, he left Almack's to his niece and her husband, Mr. Willis, who continued to run it and seems to have passed it onto other descend-ants, as the club was renamed "Willis's Rooms" in 1871.

## Lord Palmerston

Mentioned above in Emily Cowper's entry, Henry John Temple, 3rd Viscount Palmerston (1784-1865) was a British statesman, serving as Prime Minister twice (from 1855-1858 and from 1859-1865), as War Secretary, and as Foreign Secretary. He was charming, intelligent, and handsome and something of a ladies' man (as can be seen from the number of Lady Patronesses he conducted *amours* with), but remained single until the love of his life, Emily Cowper, was widowed. Their subsequent marriage, lasting until his death, was (according to observers) one of "perpetual courtship."

Here's a sneak preview of the next story in The Ladies of Almack's series, *An Event at Epsom,* coming on August 2!

# AN EVENT AT EPSOM

## Chapter One

*En route to Epsom, Surrey*
*Mid-June, 1810*

"I have always wondered why they call them 'downs,'" Maria Sefton said, gazing at the rolling green countryside outside the carriage window. "Don't they go up as much as down? Indeed," she said, warming to her subject, "since they must go up in order to go down, why are they not called 'ups'? It seems very arbitrary."

Across from her, Annabel smiled. It was an exceedingly Maria-ish thing to say. "I don't know, but 'Epsom Downs' sounds much better than 'Epsom Ups,'" she replied.

"That's true." Maria's brow wrinkled. "I shall ask Derby about it when I see him. If anyone would know, it is he."

"Except I believe there are downs elsewhere and not just in Surrey," Annabel couldn't resist adding.

"Oh, dear. That does complicate the question."

"Does Lord Derby know we're coming?" Georgiana Bathurst, seated next to Maria, asked. She'd spoken barely a word since they'd left London, and had spent the intervening hours wearing a slight frown as she gazed fixedly at nothing. Annabel had feared she was carriage-sick, but they'd not needed to pause for her to cast up her accounts in the hedgerow. The only other conclusion to be drawn was that something was troubling her.

"Of course he is expecting me. I don't think he knows you're coming," Maria replied. "This investigation was Mr. Almack's idea, not Derby's. However, I am certain he would be monstrous glad of our help, if it turns out that there is indeed something not-quite-right going on here."

They were on their way to Epsom, site of two of the most hotly-contested (and lucrative) horse-races in England—the Derby and the Oaks Stakes—which had somehow also become one of the more popular events of the season. Mr. Almack's death had not blunted his keen interest in the Sport of Kings, and a curious story had come to him that made a man—er, ghost—of his experience sit up and take notice.

"Speaking of peculiar, there's something verra odd going on in racing circles," he'd announced at Monday's Lady Patronesses meeting after they had discussed the incident with the Potamides at Eton. "Something that I think you ladies might want to look at."

"Odd in what way?" Sally had asked, taking a fresh leaf of paper and dipping her pen.

The tale Mr. Almack had recounted had indeed been an odd one. Earlier that spring a new filly had appeared on the local race circuit around Newmarket and had won almost every race she ran. Her owner, a Sir Oswald Broxley, was known amongst the gentlemen of the turf as a not-very-successful amateur breeder and trainer. With this horse, however, his luck finally seemed to have turned the corner. When asked, Sir Oswald was not forthcoming about Maharahnee's origins; he would only smile smugly and say that she'd been bred and born on his family's estate.

Dorothea had snorted. "I do not see what is so mysterious about this as to be of interest to us."

"I'm getting to that part," Mr. Almack replied, a little testily. "What is of interest is that she's a verra intelligent horse; as far as anyone can see her jockey is more or less along for the ride whilst she chooses her own path. She also doesna seem to need to rest; she'll run one day and be at a race twenty miles away the next day, ready to go."

They'd all been silent, absorbing that. Sir Oswald was not known to possess a wagon capable of carrying horses, so how could this Maharahnee win a race one afternoon then walk twenty miles to the next one in less than a day and be ready once again to race?

Sally had finally spoken. "Either this Sir Oswald has managed to tame a kelpie—"

"*Can* one tame a kelpie?" Frances interrupted, wide-eyed.

"Nae, it canna be. It's a filly, and most all kelpies are male." Mr. Almack sounded amused. "'Twould be difficult to hide that."

"Oh. Yes, it would." Frances blushed. "I beg your pardon, Sally. Pray go on."

Sally nodded and went on, "—or some poor horse has been put under a compulsion spell. I expect it must be that." She turned to Mr. Almack's empty—or rather, apparently empty—chair. "I presume the horse's owner is making a tidy profit in winnings?"

"Aye, he is. And from all accounts, he needs it—the man's known to have the worst luck—or judgment—in three counties." Mr. Almack's tone made it clear which he thought was the case. "The Oaks Stakes—it's a race for three-year-old fillies, ye ken—comes up at the end of this week at Epsom, and if there's somethin' not natural about one of the competitors, I think we should look into it."

"I expect we should." Sally looked down the table. "Maria, this would seem to be a matter you would best be able to get to the bottom of. Will you take it on?"

"It would not be any trouble at all, as Sefton and I had already planned to go to Epsom on

Wednesday to stay with Lord Derby," Maria said. "If Georgiana isn't otherwise occupied, perhaps she would come as well. Georgiana?"

"Yes, I suppose, if my rheumatism does not confine me to bed." Georgiana sighed. "And so long as it isn't a kelpie."

And so Maria and Georgiana were undertaking the investigation, with Annabel to assist as needed with gathering information. A footman had been dispatched at once to secure accommodation for them at an inn in the vicinity. Annabel had doubted he would—rooms would be almost impossible to find in Epsom at this late hour. Fortunately for them he was an engaging fellow, and the fund Mr. Almack had left for the Lady Patronesses' expenses a deep one; comfortable rooms had been found for Annabel and Georgiana at the Horse and Oak, conveniently close to the racecourse. Maria of course would be a guest at Lord Derby's house.

Annabel watched the green hills ebb and swell through the dust raised by the carriages in front of them—the closer they got to Epsom, the more crowded the roads had grown—and could not help wishing that she could have spent these days alone. On Monday this had seemed as if it would be an amusing investigation to help with. But that had been Monday. Now it was Wednesday—and her life had turned upside down in the intervening day.

Not a great deal had actually *happened* on Tuesday, aside from the prodigious amount of shopping she'd done with Mama which had cast her maid Winters into transports of joy. The part of

Tuesday that had plunged her into such confusion had been, outwardly, a small one: the brief exchange she'd had with the Marquis of Quinceton whilst they drove in Hyde Park that afternoon.

Such a little thing on the face of it, those few words. Except that they had forced her to confront the fact that she *did* regard him differently than she had three months before—that she now found him more than a little attractive, more than a little. . . love-worthy.

When he had asked her—shyly, almost (fancy the haughty Marquis of Quinceton being shy!)—to call him Quin, she'd darted a glance at his face. There was a warmth in his eyes that made her look away again before he could see her discomposure. And his softly voiced, "Please?" had nearly undone her; she'd whispered, "Yes, Quin," so quietly that there should have been no way he had heard her above the jangle of harness and the clop of his horses' hooves.

But he'd heard her. And now—what?

Oh, the immediate "what" was simple: to investigate this miracle horse for the Lady Patronesses. It was a shame, however, that she would have to help conduct the investigation with a brain that had apparently regressed to that of a green girl in her debut season engaging in her first flirtation.

If only there had been time to confide in Mama; she'd clearly grasped the situation with Quin at Eton. Heavens, she'd shamelessly arranged their meeting in Hyde Park yesterday. But there had been no chance to talk, as Papa had invited friends to join them for dinner last night at the hotel and then he and Mama had left early this morning to return to Belsever Magna. She would have to wrestle with this alone.

Very well, then. Wrestle she would.

Life as a widow—even if not a wealthy one—was in many ways very agreeable. Emily thought she should enjoy herself more and take a lover, and indeed the idea was tempting after her less-than-satisfying marriage to Freddy. But while other women seemed to be able to do so even when they weren't widowed, she couldn't contemplate the idea with Emily's pretty insouciance. She did not long for dalliance, but for love.

And if she found a man she could wholeheartedly love, well. . . men had an unfortunate habit of expecting to control the women in their lives, as she well knew. Was she prepared to give up her life of relative freedom and subject herself once more to the tyranny of a man, deliciously tempting that might be if the tyrant were someone as attractive as Quin?

In which case, a few days away from London was probably a good thing after all. She would have time and distance to mull over her feelings about Quin—unless he had been serious when he'd suggested that he might look in at the races. Then again, finding her amongst the thirty or forty thousand other race-goers would not be an easy task. So she could assume she'd have a quiet few days to contemplate—

"I suppose our first task will be to find this Maharahnee as quickly as possible, so that

Georgiana and I can talk to her before the race on Saturday," Maria said, breaking into her thoughts. "You two can try to discover where she is stabled, assuming she's gained enough of a reputation. Your being at a local inn is very helpful."

"That makes sense." Annabel gave herself a mental shake. She and Georgiana could ask innocent questions, and if required, she herself would do some more covert information gathering—eavesdropping, to be blunt—safely concealed in a shadow. But if all this investigation required was finding out where the horse was kept and Maria having a heart-to-heart talk with it, she would probably not have much to do. In fact..."I wish Emily were here. We could simply turn her loose on this Sir Oswald and find out exactly what is going on."

"Annabel, you know we require solid evidence of wrong-doing. Emily's skills are useful to shape the direction of investigations, but we never rely exclusively on what she reads," Maria said, a little reprovingly. "And anyway, Dorothea wanted her to help investigate that odd business with the ghost and the new gas lamps in Pall Mall."

"*Those* things." Georgiana shook her head. "There's something off about that."

"Gas lamps?" Annabel asked. "I'm not convinced about them either, but I can see how useful they might be for street lighting."

"Not just the gas lamps. Have you not noticed how busy we are this year? When in past years have we had more than one investigation happening at any time, or had them so close together as we have this year?"

Annabel blinked. "I don't know. This is only my second year as a Lady Patroness. Is this year busier than usual?"

"I hadn't really noticed," Maria said slowly. "But I do believe you are correct, Georgiana—this is probably the busiest it's been since the nineties."

The nineties, when war with France had first kindled then blazed. Annabel glanced at the faces of the other women and guessed their thoughts were flowing on similar lines. "You don't think that the French—" she began.

"That the French might be responsible for how busy we've been of late?" Maria said. "I don't know. I don't see how the situations involving Mr. Marjoribanks or the Ronderleys could have anything to do with the war. The Sirens are perhaps questionable; Aunt Molpe may not have told us everything about how they came to be in England, but I doubt it."

"But the Potamides—and the gas lamp incidents Dorothea and Emily are investigating. . .?" Georgiana said.

"Frances will be making discreet inquiries into the Potamides," Annabel said. "If there's any possibility that Lord Rossing might not—not be loyal, surely she'll find out *something*."

"Yes, and I shall be interested to hear what she finds out," Georgiana replied.

After that, they all fell silent while the carriage moved slowly with the stream of traffic flowing toward Epsom. Annabel couldn't suppress a faint shiver; joking about sending Angelique Ronderley to Paris to sabotage Napoleon's pictures in the *Musée Napoléon* was one thing. But contemplating that an Englishman such as Lord Rossing might be doing the Emperor's bidding here in his own country—and engaging in activities that might have sent her son and his Eton classmates to a watery grave in the Thames. . . she shivered again. Thank heavens Frances was looking into it.

*An Event at Epsom* will be out on August 2, 2022.

# About the Author

Marissa Doyle graduated from Bryn Mawr College and went on to graduate school intending to be an archaeologist, but somehow got distracted. Eventually she figured out what she was *really* supposed to be doing and started writing. She's channeled her inner history geekiness into a successful young adult historical fantasy series and continues happily to write fantasy of various types for teens and adults. She lives in her native Massachusetts with her family, including a bossy but adorable pet rabbit, and loves quilting, gardening, and collecting antiques. Please visit her at her website, www.marissadoyle.com, and at her history blog, www.nineteenteen.com.

To keep up with new releases, news, and other fun stuff, sign up for Marissa's newsletter:
 https://marissadoylenewsletter.link/

# About Book View Café

Book View Café is an author-owned cooperative of professional writers publishing in a variety of genres, from fantasy to romance, mystery, and science fiction as well as select non-fiction.

Book View Café authors include New York Times and USA Today bestsellers; Nebula, Hugo, and Philip K Dick Award winners; World Fantasy Award, Campbell Award, and Rita Award nominees; and nominees and winners of multiple other publishing awards.

To keep informed of new releases, specials, and other news, sign up for Book View Café's monthly newsletter at www.bookviewcafe.com.

Made in United States
Orlando, FL
27 November 2022